Prai
Secrets of Roma.

"Jezmina and Paulina have written a thorough, insightful, and conversational guide to fortune-telling, yes—but more importantly, to the Romani psyche. Most of us grow up straddling two cultures, and it effects how we think, how we perceive, and how we move through space. Readers will gain a solid grounding in Romani divination practices and Romani spirituality. While much of our culture remains closed to outsiders, Jezmina and Paulina continue their mission of building bridges between the Romani and other cultures, and helping others appreciate our beautiful, diverse traditions. *Laċhi buti, phenja!* (Good work, sisters!)"

—Caren Gussoff Sumption, author of
So Quick Bright Things Come to Confusion and *Three Songs for Roxy*

"Potent and revelatory, *Secrets of Romani Fortune-Telling* is a groundbreaking book that illuminates the often-overlooked history, diversity, and resilience of the Romani diaspora and Romani divinatory practices."

—Kristen J. Sollée, author of *Witches, Sluts, Feminists*

"*Secrets of Romani Fortune-Telling* is a beautifully written guide for anyone wanting to practice the art of divination, but it's so much more. Authors Jezmina and Paulina pull back the curtain, inviting us into their hearts and homes to share a little slice of magic born out of centuries of resilience."

—Paige Vanderbeck, host *of The Fat Feminist Witch*
podcast and author of *Witchcraft for Emotional Wisdom*

"Our obsession with fortune-telling is timeless. We all want clarity about our present circumstances and accurate glimpses of the future, but the methods used to discern these mysteries are often fleeting or not easily accessible. In *Secrets of Romani Fortune-Telling*, readers are given a key that unlocks the doors to those mysteries. A comprehensive exploration of a fascinating and deeply mystical culture, this rare book also sheds light on the Romani world and its treasured traditions, centuries-old customs, and magical methods. How can we strengthen our intuition? What can we learn about our fates through palmistry? From reading tea and coffee leaves to understanding the hidden symbols of our dreams, this revelatory book plumbs the depths of divination with expert guidance and care. In these pages are practical exercises and techniques that will enhance the knowledge of both the seasoned practitioner and newly curious seeker. *Secrets of Romani Fortune-Telling* is a wise and wonderful addition to every bookshelf."

—Antonio Pagliarulo, author of *The Evil Eye*

"Jezmina and Paulina have created a beautiful portrait of Romani life and culture highlighting historical aspects, members of the community, and personal narratives while giving everyday advice to keep your mind, body, and spirit balanced and healthy. Thoughtful and inclusive *Secrets of Romani Fortune-Telling* is a comprehensive guide to tarot, palmistry, dream work, tasseography, and spiritual health with an emphasis on reverence and respect for the community and one's elders and ancestors. This book is a love letter to Romani culture and an invitation to understanding more about it."

—Katelan Foisy, artist for *The Hoodoo Tarot* and
Sibyls Oraculum: Oracle of the Black Doves of Africa

Secrets of
ROMANI FORTUNE-TELLING

Divining with Tarot, Palmistry, Tea Leaves, and More

Jezmina Von Thiele and Paulina Stevens

WEISER BOOKS

This edition first published in 2024 by Weiser Books, an imprint of
Red Wheel/Weiser, LLC
With offices at:
65 Parker Street, Suite 7
Newburyport, MA 01950
www.redwheelweiser.com

Permission to quote from Raine Geoghegan's poem "Lucy the Dukkerer," from
the poetry collection *The Talking Stick: O Pookering Kosh* (Salmon Poetry, 2022)
kindly granted by Salmon Poetry, Cliffs of Moher, County Clare, Ireland.

ISBN: 978-1-57863-858-1
Library of Congress Cataloging-in-Publication Data available upon request.

Cover illustration by Anna Rabko
Family photos courtesy of the authors
Interior by Steve Amarillo / Urban Design, LLC
Typeset in Adobe Caslon, Almendra, and Amarante

Printed in the United States of America
IBI
10 9 8 7 6 5 4 3 2 1

To Romanistan and all of Sara la Kali's children.

Contents

Acknowledgments

We are both so grateful to so many people. Thank you to our editor Judika Illes, to Peter Turner for finding us, and to Weiser for believing in us. Thank you to Anna Rabko of Happy Borders for her beautiful cover and artwork, and to everyone who contributed to this book, Pierce and Raquel Horvath of Dead Scared Entertainment, Frances Roberts Reilly, Raine Geoghegan, Aurora Luna, Ylvadroma Marzanna Radziszewski, Katelan Foisy, April Wall, Oksana Marafioti, Jennileen Joseph, Alice Johnson, Ethel Brooks. . . . Thank you, Erik Decker, for checking our grammar and teaching us both more about our language. We're also very grateful to our *Romanistan* podcast crew, editor Cherub and musician Viktor Pachas, artist Elijah Vardo, every single Romanistan guest, and our listeners and supporters, as well as the *Foretold* podcast crew and listeners. We also have some personal acknowledgments to share.

Paulina's Acknowledgments

Thank you to my beautiful girls, Allison and Alina, for pushing me to be the best version of myself, allowing me to love and cherish you every day, and making life worth living. Thank you, Jezmina for taking me on this journey with you, always believing in me, hearing me out, and giving the best advice. You inspire me and so many others, and I am excited for our future adventures. Thank you, Cherub, and Victor, our dream team. Thank you, Mom and Nicole, for keeping the hookah and tea warm. Thank you to my paternal Papo, both of my grandmothers and my great-grandmother Duda, RIP. Thank you, Mia, Nicole W., Leah, and Cami, my best friends. Thank you, Angelina, Arián, Gina, Veronica, Natalya, Faith Pinho, Bethanie, MAV, Kiki, Ylva, and the folks at Dead Scared Entertainment. Thank you, Dr. V, Rachel H., and Jamie G.F. for all the support. Thank you to the city of Los Angeles for being my healing ground and birthplace. Thank you to the haters, I couldn't have done this without you, of course. Much love to my past, current, and future clients.

Jezmina's Acknowledgments

Thank you to my grandma for teaching me everything and preserving your culture when so many wanted to forget, and for being one of my favorite people in the world. Thank you to my mom and Auntie Zina for all the stories and adventures, and to my dad for your support, and for connecting me to nature and his own kind of spirituality. Thank you to Bruce and Jack, you are so dear to me, and to Vickie because you are a delight. Thank you to Nona for being the matriarch, for Papa for teaching me to appreciate craft in many forms, and Auntie Susie for being my witchy Auntie with your own special traditions. And thank you to all the family I did not name, and the family I do not know. Thank you to Paulina for going on this journey with me, inspiring me, conspiring with me, and making our work fun and something to be proud of. You're like the sister I never had. Thank you to those who have helped me as I heal, especially Melinda, Matthew, Emily, Christine, Kelley, and Michael. Thank you to my all my Deadwick's and Pickwick's friends, especially Lady Rosamond, Fae, Elysian, Heathcliff, Fern, Penny, Juniper, Zinnia, Fulcanelli, and Cara. Thank you to my clients, past, present, and future. And thank you to dear friends, Miranda, Jen, Courtney, Genn, Naomi, Lauren, Sarah, Ylva, Kiki, Katlyn, Juanita, Dia, Olivia, Andrew, Diana Norma, Nina, Akin, and Gary especially. I'm blessed to have met good people everywhere I've gone, so if we're friends, or even just friendly, I'm thanking you too. Thank you to everyone at The Poetry Brothel Boston Chapter. Thank you to Victor Pachas for being the best chickadee. And thank you to many feral cats, and to Bosco, the best ghost dog, and Lily, the best bad dog.

Illustration by Anna Rabko

Welcome to Fortune-Telling

We're Your Friendly Neighborhood Gypsies

Imagine you were born into an ancient tradition of divination that has been passed down from generation to generation for your culture's survival. Perhaps, reader, you were. In which case, you know the heaviness, responsibility, and resilience braided into such a lineage. If you cannot relate or cannot imagine, then come with us into a world that is unknown to most.

Someone comes into your shop, announced by the tinkling bells you hung on the handle for protection. You call out welcome and tell them you're offering "tarot, palm, tea-leaf, and coffee readings," and other holistic services. You see the guest's eyes take in walls draped with tapestries and floors covered in Turkish rugs, and the stained-glass window you had custom-made to add color. A warm but subtle light emanates from an assortment of lamps swathed in bright scarves, as well as the candles you blessed, oiled, and lit this morning along with the rolled incense on your shop's altar. You gesture over to the apothecary lined with herbs, spices, teas, and supplements. Some are from your culture, some not, but then Romani culture has both borrowed and given so much all over the world that sometimes the lines blur even for you. The guest walks once around the shop, glancing at the hand-dipped candles, incense cones, oils and elixirs, statues, herb bundles, and crystals. You wonder if they know who you are, what the sign "Romani Holistic" means outside your shop, if they have any fears, or even hatred towards Gypsies.

"Let me know if you have any questions," you say.

"How much is a reading?" they ask.

You lead them over to a comfortable chair and sit across from them. You shuffle the deck of cards on the round table in front of you, decorated with a mangano calcite to enhance empathy, and a black moonstone for grounding and spiritual protection. You skipped the small talk. That's something you love about this job. You cut right to what's important. You just met, but the guest is crying in front of you, telling you they just feel so lost. You offer them a tissue from a marble box, and you feel a wave of compassion for this perfect stranger and shift that energy into the cards as you're shuffling, asking them, your ancestors, your spirit guides, and maybe *O Del*, or *Devel* (God), or whichever gods you choose, to help you give them some answers so they can find their footing and take their own confident steps out again.

How did you even get here? Pulling cards with a stranger, telling them about their life? The real question is, how could you not? You've tried to put them away, the cards, the teacups, the porcelain diagrams of secrets written on the palms, but they call you. They call your blood and bones. That's why you are here.

To understand the true art of Romani fortune-telling, and the secrets of intuition, we will share some spiritual techniques and business acumen, but more than that, we will share our beliefs, culture, history, trauma, resilience, and our stories. All of these make up the much misunderstood, maligned, and misrepresented practice of Romani divination. No one really knows what it means to be a Gypsy except the Gypsies themselves, and even among us that can mean different things. We are just two people who have come together to share our little slice of Romanistan, and what we love about it, and what we wish for our future.

In this book, Paulina and Jezmina will introduce you to the history of the Romani people and their infamous relationship to fortune-telling, as well as the labor of divination methods, tools, and techniques that Roma created, adapted, or popularized. As fortune-telling is both a job and a spiritual practice for Roma, we are particularly excited to share tips on how to use intuition as a practical tool for survival and how to emulate the professional polish that Roma have perfected over the centuries.

We share our knowledge from personal experiences of being raised to be fortune-tellers, but it's important to us that readers realize we are speaking only from our experiences, as we do not speak for all Roma, nor do we want to. We will, however, share additional resources here and on *Romanistan* podcast for you to explore.

At the same time, it's important to understand that a lot of Romani culture is closed to outsiders. There is much that we cannot and will not share. Some of what we share has already made its way into mainstream culture through centuries of coexistence. Some of our practices and beliefs overlap with or parallel other cultures, and some may be unique to us, but we will not publicize anything that is considered truly secret or sacred. We also acknowledge that, in the movement toward better Romani representation, we as Roma need to share more of our culture than many of us are used to in order to help people understand us, support us, respect us, and learn how to avoid cultural appropriation and instead engage in cultural exchange. In the spirit of sharing, we will tell you a little about how we each came to fortune-telling.

Paulina's Story

I was raised within my *Muchwaya* Romani family's fortune-telling and wellness traditions. Muchwaya is the name of a Romani *vitsa*, or clan, who mostly settled in Serbia. My family's bloodline is Romani, but also consists of South Asian, Middle Eastern, and Eastern European descent because of our travels. My parents owned spiritual shops throughout San Francisco, Los Angeles, and the central coast of California, and I was taught tarot, palmistry, coffee readings, energy healing, and how to work with teas and spices to balance the body and spirit. Growing up poor, my mother would cook every day and shop at the farmer's market in front of our home; our home doubled as the town's local metaphysical shop, because we usually lived in our shops. From an early age, I was taught the benefit of eating whole foods, grown locally. Holistic health and spirituality were the only things I was allowed to do as a child and young adult.

Growing up in my community, I was isolated from the outside world. Our elders believed this was necessary to preserve our ways and rich cultural traditions. There are countless aspects to my heritage that I am truly in love with, including our language, cuisine, arts, music, and passion. I believe we must fight to keep our traditions too, and perhaps learn to adapt some others, but I also needed to strike out on my own path, and that meant breaking the unwritten laws my people have practiced for thousands of years. I am the subject of the *Los Angeles Times* podcast series *Foretold*, which tells the story of my decision to leave my arranged marriage and traditional community and navigate a new life, walking between the Romani world and the non-Romani world.

In my professional life, I combined my family's way of traditional Romani divination and fortune-telling with modern whole-body wellness techniques. Inspired by the holistic health movement and my life experience, Romani Holistic, my California new age shop and private practice, was born. I earned a wellness coaching certificate and later began collaborating with nutritionists and herbalists to create comprehensive plans for clients that cater to body and soul. At Romani Holistic, we focus on addressing the physical, mental, emotional, social, and spiritual components of health. We continue to use herb, spice, and plant remedies, as well as the same fortune-telling and spiritual guidance methods of my ancestors. Along with being a holistic practitioner, I am currently a student of biotechnology, and I love studying where science and spirituality meet. I hope to share our methods and continue learning along the way.

In the *Los Angeles Times* podcast series *Foretold*, I explain how because I was only allowed to be a fortune-teller, once I left my small community, I briefly gave up fortune-telling, divination, and most cultural practices I grew up with, and at the time, resented it altogether. I blamed all of our practices for the hardships I dealt with, such as arranged teen marriage, exposure to crime, being taken out of elementary school, and other intergenerational trauma. I didn't want my daughters to experience the same cycle, and when I became aware of it, I felt that my whole life and spiritual practice were a lie. While taking time to heal, I poured myself into education, the history of my people, and the origins of our practices. I came to understand the difference between culture and the symptoms of systemic racism.

Obviously, I have grown from that experience, and I understand that Romani crime is not inherent to our culture, but a result of oppression and internalized prejudice and sexism. I couldn't let go of my connection to my culture, our holistic way of living, our superstitions, and deep-rooted spirituality, no matter how hard I tried. I came back to my practice stronger and more passionate.

Paulina's maternal great-grandparents with their family

Paulina's paternal grandparents and family

Jezmina's Story

I am from a mixed and assimilated family, meaning that I did not grow up in a traditional community, and only my maternal grandmother is Romani. Her vitsa is called the *Sinti*, a subgroup of Roma that mostly settled in Germany, Austria, and parts of Italy. My grandmother grew up in Germany during World War II (1939-1945), when Roma and Sinti were violently persecuted as targeted ethnic groups during the Holocaust.

World War II shattered many Romani and Sinti families through execution and imprisonment, and many were forced to run and hide. My family survived through a mixture of hiding and assimilating through extreme measures that even I don't know all the details of. Before the war, my great-great-grandmother, Mathilde, danced and read fortunes in her family tradition under the stage surname that she adopted, Von Thiele; a name that is not Romani but indicates royalty. She was essentially branding herself, making the most of the stereotype of the "Gypsy princess" as part of her performance. She and her husband taught my grandmother and her siblings everything they could about their culture and trades in secret.

My grandmother came to the United States after the war was over because Germany was still an extremely unsafe place for Roma, Jewish people, and other persecuted minorities to be, and even difficult for many white German citizens too. She married an American soldier she barely knew and traveled to America on a ship, alone, speaking no English. It gave my grandmother an opportunity to reinvent herself in a new country.

My grandmother was proud of being Romani, but, due to prejudice, she felt she had to keep it a secret in the US too, even from her own children until they were more grown and could be trusted to be quiet about it. My grandmother told fortunes in the neighborhood to make friends and do what she loved, but it was a secret homage to her family. She was very poor but she didn't take money for fortune-telling because she was afraid of being perceived as a Gypsy, but she accepted food or coffee in exchange. This is one of the reasons my grandmother didn't encourage her children to tell fortunes, though she did teach them some things. Either way, she said my mother and auntie weren't cut out for fortune-telling, because my mother only saw misfortune and because my auntie was too anxious. Both are bad for business. So my mother and auntie worked with horses, another popular trade, and had a number of other jobs.

My grandmother passed away in 2023, and we were very close. She said that when I was born, she realized that if she didn't pass on our culture, it would be lost. She started training me to be a fortune-teller when I was four or five years old through dream interpretation, ancestor veneration, plant and animal relationships, and meditative prayer, and the divination tools themselves. It was the most joyful part of my childhood. She had me reading professionally at parties when I was a preteen. She taught me everything she remembered from her own fragmented relationship with Romani culture. I am very aware of both the cultural loss but also the privilege that comes from being assimilated—it is not the same at all as growing up traditionally and immersed in community. At the same time, many folks of Romani descent are mixed, assimilated, and navigating what that all means, so I'm sharing my experience as a mixed and assimilated person of Romani heritage. But this too is part of the diverse Romani experience.

I offer tarot, palm, and tea-leaf readings in person and online, as well as mentorship. My sessions are conversational and goal oriented. I want to help you shake off what's holding you back, discover your potential, and move down helpful paths to get you where you want to be. I love reading for any kind of client who finds me, and I specialize in working with artists, writers, performers, or folks who are looking to access more self-expression and creativity in their day-to-day lives. I studied English and creative writing, and have worked in performance art, multimedia arts, and taught as an adjunct college professor and a middle school humanities teacher. I edit books and coach writers and other creators, and I've published poetry, fiction, and nonfiction under the name Jessica Reidy as well. I began using the stage name, Jezmina Von Thiele, in 2014 because fortune-telling and performance work were at odds with the university jobs that I was pursuing, and I kept using it. Jezmina is a combination of nicknames my mother had for me as a kid and the name of my Auntie Zina, whom I adored. I borrow Von Thiele from my great-great-grandmother Mathilde in honor of her perseverance and success.

I have also had training in trauma sensitivity through my work and training as a yoga teacher through Kripalu and the Trauma Center at JRI, and while I am not a therapist, and I'm not trying to be, I enjoy supporting folks working through their trauma as one facet of a holistic approach to healing. I'm not afraid to witness the hardest parts of the human experience and I consider it a privilege to hold compassionate space for clients.

Jezmina's great-great-grandmother Mathilde

Jezmina's grandmother Christa

Romanistan

For us, Romanistan is an imaginary land for the Romani people to belong to, wherever you are in the world, and it is also the name of the podcast we started on February 14, 2021, Valentine's Day. So, welcome to Romanistan! We're your friendly neighborhood Gypsies! Romanistan is our love letter to Romani culture. We interview Romani people from different backgrounds about all the amazing things they do. Sometimes we have "international relations" guests who are not Roma, but who are doing things we think the community would love to know about. We celebrate Romani identity and outcast culture, and practice good diplomatic relations with other marginalized communities.

We love the rebels, and the outcasts of the outcasts, who are living their truth, even if it challenges tradition. We both feel very strongly that Romani culture, like all cultures, needs to continue to evolve. We consider ourselves an intersectional feminist platform and gender liberationists, and we advocate for positive change in the world and within our own community. We speak out against the hard issues the Romani community faces, such as the normalization of domestic violence, crime, sexism, arranged teen marriage, the exclusion of LGBTQIA+ Roma, and the like. If we pretend that these problems don't exist, they will not change. Sometimes we are criticized for reinforcing stereotypes when we highlight issues within the community,, but we don't believe these issues are inherently Romani. They are symptoms of any culture oppressed by systemic racism and the patriarchy. We are also pro-peace and anti-colonization, and as such believe that Romanistan is a state of mind and needn't be an actual physical state with borders in order for us to have representation, though we do need to be recognized as a stateless ethnic group to better fight for human rights. Our ideal Romanistan is an inclusive global community of Roma and related groups unified by culture, activism, and mutual love and support.

We're not exactly "model Roma," and we're not trying to be, and what does that even mean? Embracing the rebel or outcast archetype is positive and empowering for us. Jezmina identifies as queer and nonbinary, is disabled, and uses they/she pronouns, is mixed, and grew up assimilated. Paulina left her arranged teen marriage and was shunned by her community, and she has two daughters she's raising to be strong feminists like her. We're both domestic violence and child abuse survivors, and have been criticized for speaking out about it, but we share because as we heal ourselves, we heal others too.

We love the traditions that give us strength and solidarity, and we love honoring our roots and seeing culture grow and thrive. *Romanistan* podcast is for everyone who loves and supports Roma and related groups, and anyone who feels like a misfit and wants to uplift others to create a beautiful community. We feature pioneers in culture, fashion, art, literature, music, activism, cuisine, and everything good. We adore the intersections of gender, sexuality, spirituality, ability, and identity. We cover all topics, from the difficult to the glorious. You can find *Romanistan* anywhere you get podcasts, and at *romanistanpodcast.com.*

CHAPTER 1

Romani Fortune-Telling History and Present Day

Who Can Say Gypsy?

The word "Gypsy" evokes a sexy, mystical, even dangerous archetype that has been perpetuated for nearly as long as the Romani people have existed. "Gypsy" is a slur and misnomer that refers to the Romani people, and sometimes refers to Travellers and other marginalized historically nomadic groups that may or may not be related to Roma. As such, it should not be appropriated or used by gadje, non-Roma, or others to whom the term does not apply. However, Romani people, Travellers, and related groups are free to reclaim the word "Gypsy," or use it or shun it however they like. Some Roma do refer to themselves as Travellers too, but there is also a separate group of people, Irish Travellers, a persecuted ethnic group of Irish descent, also known as Pavees or Mincéirs, and sometimes they are referred to as Gypsies too even though they are not related to Roma.

It's a little confusing, but stay with us. In the UK and Ireland, the word "Gypsy" tends to be used more neutrally because it is a legal category, and some Roma and Travellers like this, and some do not. We're not looking to police the way that Roma, Travellers, and related groups refer to themselves. We support you no matter which terms you prefer. We want to educate non-Roma that the word "Gypsy" is very charged and is not something you to can use however you like, or appropriate, exploit, brand, or otherwise profit off of, or wield as a slur. We both reclaim "Gypsy" because it's the word we grew up with, and it is the right of any marginalized group to reclaim words that refer to them if they want to.

The stereotypes of the "magical Gypsy" the "criminal Gypsy," the "promiscuous Gypsy," and so on have been tools of oppression and dehumanization for centuries. This is why many Roma prefer that gadje, or non-Roma, do not use the term "Gypsy" to refer to themselves or anything else, even if there are also some good associations with the word. If a Romani person, Traveller, or a member of a related group explicitly asks you to refer to them as a Gypsy, that's fine. But otherwise, leave that word to us.

Who Are the Roma?

To clarify a point that often confuses people, Roma are not Romanians or Romans. Opinions differ, but many agree that Roma is the noun, and Romani is the adjective (e.g., The Roma, and the Romani people), and sometimes it is spelled Rroma and Rromani for added clarification, or Romany in the UK and Ireland. Roma are a diasporic ethnic group who originated in the region of Northern India and Pakistan around the 10th and 11th centuries CE. To be diasporic means to be dispersed, and refers to any ethnic group that is scattered across regions that are not their origin.

According to Romani linguists and historians such as Dr. Ian Hancock, those early Roma were likely low caste Indians and other migrants who were rounded up as an army to fight the Ghaznavid Empire, an invading Muslim army, on behalf of the Hindus in India. The Ghaznavid campaigns in India lasted from 973-1027 CE, and the armies fighting for India were allowed to camp away from the battleground with their families. India lost the war, and by that time, an entire culture of people had formed in those camps outside the battlefield, and many were captured and taken prisoner by the opposition. Others who escaped likely returned to India, but some would have traveled West of their own free will. Since the new Romani people moved West, by choice or by force, they have been persecuted and marginalized, enslaved and hunted, and continuously misrepresented over the centuries.

Roma arrived in Europe in waves around the 1300s and 1400s and were met by hostile locals most places they went. It was the tail end of the Crusades, and they were dark-skinned people who worshiped many gods and spoke a Sanskrit-based language. You can imagine that didn't go over well. Roma were enslaved for over five hundred years in present-day Romania, and in the principalities of Wallachia and Moldavia, from the 1370s (though possibly earlier) until 1856, when slavery was abolished in the last remaining principality.

Romani people, coming from India, were ethnically distinct from Romanians, with darker skin and different customs, and this was their excuse for forcing Roma into chattel slavery. This is when the concept of the "criminal Gypsy" was born as justification for this gross mistreatment. Because this period of slavery was occurring concurrently with the transatlantic slave trade, the first Roma arrived in America during the 16th century as slaves sent to work in plantations. When Roma were freed in Romania, they were paid no reparations, and this history is rarely taught or acknowledged, even in Romania. For more on the history of Romani slavery, see the work of Margareta Matache, Delia Grigore, Ian Hancock, and Elena Marushiakova. Aside from enslavement, in other European countries, Roma were also deported, tortured, hunted, and otherwise oppressed.

There were multiple genocides of Roma throughout the centuries, and one that is otherwise well-documented but still overlooked is the genocide of Roma and Sinti (1935-1945) during the Holocaust, or the National Socialist genocide. The Romani word for this genocide is Samudaripen, a neologism first coined by linguist Marcel Courthiade in the 1970s, translating to "mass murder." Readers might be familiar with the Romani word Porajmos, sometimes used to refer to the Holocaust, which means devouring or destruction, but because of the word's other definitions and connotations, it is no longer the preferred term, so Samudaripen is more appropriate. At least one million Roma and Sinti were murdered during Samudaripen, in death camps and through other means, but experts estimate the numbers are much higher, since many

Romani families were executed upon discovery and their deaths were not documented. The Romani and Sinti loss during the Holocaust is routinely excluded, but projects and organizations like RomArchive and Dikh He Na Bister are working hard to ensure that this history is not forgotten. While Samudaripen is over, neofascism is still very much alive, and Roma and Sinti are still oppressed by the far right and are victims of hate crimes today.

In these ways, over the centuries, Roma were forced into the margins of society again and again throughout history, and so to survive Roma worked trades they had taken with them from India and West Asia, like fortune-telling, metalsmithing, performing, agricultural work, animal training, leather work, horse trading, lace making, and other jobs that could be practiced on the run. Roma's nomadism was born of persecution, not wanderlust. These trades were practiced out of survival, and still are. At the same time, Romani people were able to contribute to society, find allies, and persist. Some traditional Romani jobs diminished over time with the advancements in technology, or transformed, like horse trading became car trading for many. Roma work many different jobs today, some traditional, some not. There are Romani doctors, lawyers, teachers, musicians, chefs, social workers, and so on. Many Roma are settled and no longer travel, but some still live a life on the road. Some are more assimilated in gadje culture (non-Roma culture), and some live very separate from gadje.

Despite this admirable resilience, Roma are still violently persecuted and fight for basic human rights worldwide, and continue to face employment, education, housing, and healthcare discrimination. Roma are the largest ethnic minority in Europe; they are still segregated in many countries and face much higher levels of imprisonment, poverty, human trafficking, and police brutality than white citizens. Roma are continuously denied refugee status in Europe and North America, with deadly consequences. Related groups, such as the Lom and the Dom, also face discrimination across West Asia, North Africa, and other areas. There are large populations of Roma in South and Central America that still fight for equal rights and representation, often alongside the local Indigenous people who are still fighting for their rights and land. It's the human rights crisis that most people have never heard of. For a list of Romani-run organizations, charities, programs, and educational resources, you can visit the resources list in the Appendix, and *romanistanpodcast.com*.

However, Romani culture is resilient and is preserved in our traditions, art, music, food, stories, Sanskrit-based language, literature, and other records. Romani culture is diverse and cannot be generalized. There are over 62 vitsas, or subgroups of Roma, each with variations in customs, linguistic differences, practices, and beliefs. Every culture is also made up of individuals with their own experiences, so while we have a unifying history and culture, we are still individuals with differences in perspectives and beliefs. Don't let this book be your only source on Romani culture. If this is your introduction, let this be a jumping off point for further discovery.

Roma and Fortune-Telling

The Roma's relationship to divination dates back to our origins in India and our time moving across West Asia. Cartomancy, tasseomancy, palmistry, and other types of divination have been with us for a very long time, sometimes originating with our ancestors, and sometimes adopted by them. As Roma moved West, they shared these and other types of divination they were known for wherever they went, making a living by reading door to door, in the streets, or even in little establishments. For instance, Roma were likely the first people to practice divination using the tarot cards created in Italy, originally played as a game and inspired by earlier iterations of playing cards across East Asia, Africa, and West Asia.

Depictions of Roma as fortune-tellers have been popular for centuries. Famous paintings by Regnier (1600s) and Caravaggio (1594) depicted Roma as both thieves and fortune-tellers, untrustworthy, seductive, and dangerously other. By the Victorian era in the UK, society ladies hosted fortune-telling parties and dressed up as Romani women to embody the aura of the Romani fortune-tellers who were going door to door, selling fortunes and their wares. This is also the time of the deeply problematic Charles Godfrey Leland, a self-proclaimed expert on Roma who established The Gypsy Lore Society, which exists today as a scholarly journal. Back then membership was open to white men who were very interested in Roma and who had bedded a Romani woman—consent not necessary.

This exoticization added another layer to the difficulties that Roma faced just trying to work a trade that some may have loved, but they had been more or less forced into because of persecution, poverty, and a lack of access to education and other opportunities. Fortune-telling became very trendy for non-Roma, but Roma were not treated better for it. This is true for many invaluable trades practiced by Roma—while gadje have benefitted from our work and creativity, they have not treated us as equals.

This practice of dressing up like a "Gypsy" still happens today, especially in the United States. Many people don't realize that doing so is making a caricature of a real ethnic group. This is particularly problematic because Romani fortune-tellers are disproportionately targeted by police and accused of scamming. Many present-day anti-fortune-telling laws in the US came from a history of Romani persecution, and the persecution of other BIPOC (Black, Indigenous, People of Color) groups who use their ancestral divinatory practices as survival trades as well. There are documented anti-Gypsy police task forces still active today who keep tabs on local Roma. This is why it's particularly important for non-Roma fortune-tellers to be allies to the Romani community, and allies to other ethnic groups whose divinatory practices have become more mainstream, and to use their privilege not to mock or appropriate other cultures but to elevate our communities, who have given so much to the profession.

Experiences with Discrimination

We have both been discriminated against for being Roma in different ways, both while working as fortune-tellers and just going about the world. Most of the racism we experience outside of fortune-telling has been more because we look ethnically ambiguous than for being specifically Romani, because in the United States it's usually a little easier to blend in as a Romani person than it is in Europe. However, when people do know our ethnicity, we have been spat on, yelled at, insulted, assaulted, called a Gypsy, thrown out of establishments, bullied, and so forth. We share more of these experiences on *Romanistan* podcast, but you get the idea. We asked some of our fellow Romani fortune-tellers and wellness practitioners to share their experiences with discrimination, and we share their quotes below.

I grew up in the southern United States and was told that fortune-telling is evil and witchcraft by gadje. I was also told that Romani fortune-tellers, in particular, were thieves and scam artists. Because of this, my granny would warn me to not tell anyone about my ethnicity for fear of retribution.—April Wall, author of *Reading Tarot, Reading Tea Leaves*, and *Deciphering Angel Numbers*

Sometimes gadje are fascinated with me being a Rroma practitioner, other times they make comments about me stealing their babies or money from their wallets. In some ways, it's refreshing that they are honest about their ignorance, though it's also hard to hear how much they have been indoctrinated by the lies about us from the dominant society. I try to brand myself within the context of "holistic health" to try to avoid the desperation people sometimes carry around fortune-tellers being able to "fix" their lives. I still get people who struggle taking charge of their own lives and want me to fix everything, definitely with some underlying unaware tones of "gypsy fortune-teller, please 'magic' away the pain." It's frustrating to navigate.—Jennileen Joseph, Ayurvedic naturopath and owner of Sastimos Holistic Health

To me it's empowering to continue to practice the ways of my ancestors and spirits (of various ancestry). It's more annoying I guess rather than disempowering (I will not allow other people to take my power or try to make me feel uncomfortable because they are) that as a spiritual practitioner, outside of our bubbles, be it online or in our real life safe spaces, we are seen as "devil worshipers" and are demonized. I feel like in the spiritual/witchy community there is a lack of intersectionality that addresses that these anti-witchcraft laws in the US and certain countries that have been around for many years are not an attack on the witchcraft community (as we know it today post Gardner/Crowley) but are directly tied to white supremacy that has demonized, attacked, and oppressed Romani people to make us illegal, in addition to Black and Indigenous people who practice their traditional practices, which continues to affect all groups involved from not being able to work, being denied housing, redlining, residential schools and the taking of our children. These laws were also put in place to persecute Catholics and Jewish people in America because America was founded on Protestant values. Instead, they want to connect it to just "Christians hate us witches" and it's like, those people didn't care about this until it started to affect them, and now they're making these laws that have had devastating effects on our communities about themselves. These are the same people that also have made successful businesses, written books and profited off of *our* practices that we still get demonized for.—Aurora Luna, AKA Baby Recklesss

I have lost my ability to process payments from PayPal, Square, Swipe on several occasions because of anti-fortune-telling laws. Most recently I permanently lost my website of thirteen years. I also work events and read at shops publicly and always have to do so next to gadje who are cosplaying Romani fortune-teller troupes.
—Ylvadroma Marzanna Radziszewski,
AKA Bimbo Yaga

How Roma View Fortune-Telling Today

Many Roma see divination as the art of reading human nature and administering commonsense therapy by using spiritual tools. Fortune-telling is a trade separate from healing services, blessings, and spiritual counsel that Roma perform for their own communities. Some Romani families, however, like our respective families, adapted fortune-telling to be both a spiritual art and a family trade, and have elevated the work to be more than a job. Writer, producer, director, and harpist Frances Roberts Reilly says that Romani fortune-telling "honors an ancestral heritage that's been passed down families from generation to generation and as such has the integrity and ethical values carried within it."

Frances sees fortune-telling and spirituality as intertwined as well: "I think I've reached a certain age where I have become more spiritual as I've aged. Romani spirituality for me is about sitting with contradictions and opposites until a third reality emerges. So I straddle two worldviews at the same time, a Roma way of being." Romani fortune-telling, spirituality, and experience can be many things at once for us, and it has to be. The Romani way is to be adaptable, always surviving and trying to thrive.

Not all Roma read fortunes, however, or even like fortune-telling as a practice, and certain vitsas or clans are more likely to work the trade than others. For some, fortune-telling is practiced only in times of financial desperation or need, and mostly for non-Romani clients. For that reason, being a fortune-teller can be stigmatized even among other Roma. Some Roma, especially those in academia or careers that have in some way transcended what is expected of us, look down on fortune-tellers, thinking that we reinforce negative stereotypes of Gypsies as silly mystics or even scammers.

Dr. Ethel Brooks of Rutgers University, a women's studies professor and author, spoke with us in season 3 of *Romanistan* podcast on episode 16, "Romani Feminism with Dr. Ethel Brooks." She explained that part of why fortune-telling has not been valued even among Roma is because it is often seen as women's work, and emotional labor and community care is consistently undervalued in patriarchal cultures, including ours. Dr. Brooks went on to say in our interview that she has performed fortune-telling as performance art in exhibitions by herself and alongside Romani artist Daniel Baker, and both received backlash from Romani activists for "giving Roma a bad name" or "playing into stereotypes." However, she did these fortune-telling performance pieces to explore racialized, gendered labor and exploitation.

Dr. Brooks says, "Part of the thing we need to valorize is the work that women have done across generations to sustain the community, and that reading, fortune-telling, *drabimos, dukkering*, whatever we want to call it, *is* the work that women have done to sustain their communities . . . and none of us would be here without that." Dr. Brooks continues to explain that the reason that Romani fortune-tellers are mistreated or looked down on by both Roma and gadje alike "is because it's about women's work." It's the "combination of race and gender that goes into the vilification of reading as labor, reading as practice, and reading as knowledge . . . and . . . we need to fight back . . . . This is what takes care of everyone, what feeds people, and this what takes care of the gadje who come in and need help." We can make the argument that Romani culture is not inherently patriarchal, and that sexism and gender roles have been impressed upon on us, but the fact is that Romani culture, like so many others, has a great need for improved gender equality, and we believe that honoring fortune-telling as valuable, respectable work is one small step toward equality.

Are Fortune-Tellers Witches?

It's important to understand that, in Romani culture, fortune-telling is not necessarily witchcraft, but that's not to say that some fortune-tellers aren't witches. There is a tradition of witchcraft and magic among some Roma, but it can be very divisive, and that is exactly the kind of closed practice that we will not be sharing. Some gadje wrongly assume that all Romani spirituality is witchraft. And some Roma wave off witchcraft as an old-fashioned idea rooted in superstitious stories, whereas others embody the archetype of the witch, whether that's within a specific family tradition, or a personal spiritual belief, or an artistic or political persona. Romani culture evolves, Roma adapt, and Romani women and LGBTQIA+ folks are responsible for some of our most important activist work, and some of them identify as fortune-tellers and/or witches as part of their lives, or simply as part of their activism. The symbol of the witch is empowering to some Roma who have felt outcast in society and their own communities. Increased access to technology and education has helped Romani fortune-tellers and witches expand their offerings, reach, audience, and clients. Just as the chosen family or clan (vitsa) of LGBTQIA+ and otherwise marginalized Roma has become a beacon of hope and a way to embrace their unique relationship to Romani culture, some are also unifying under the mantle of the witch. Whether it truly reflects their spiritual beliefs, or whether it's a powerful shorthand for proud difference, it's creating a fascinating artistic and cultural movement.

Romanian Roma Mihaela Drăgan, actress, musician, writer, and filmmaker, pioneered the Roma Futurism movement, and she credits inspiration to the AfroFuturism and SinoFuturism movements before it. In Roma Futurism, Drăgan recreates the Romani witch stereotype and transforms it into the Techno Witch, aka CyberWitch archetype, acknowledging the societal role that some Roma have played as witches historically, as healers, fortune-tellers, spell casters, midwives, wise people, and more, and combined this multifaceted witch with elements of sci-fi and technology.

In 2014, Drăgan founded the feminist Romani theatre troupe Giuvlipen (the Romani word for *feminism*), with Zita Moldovan, a Romani actress, television presenter, journalist, and fashion designer. One of Giuvlipen's celebrated Roma Futurist plays is called, "Romacen: The Age of the Witch," about Romani Techno Witches who use traditional magic and malware to curse fascist politicians, warp reality, and travel back in time to try to stop Samudaripen, the genocide of Roma and Sinti in WWII that is often left out of history books. The archetype of the Techno Witch is compelling artistically and politically because it subverts the gadje fantasy of "Gypsy witches" by empowering and representing aspects of traditional magic within Romani culture associated with witchcraft. The Techno Witch is brilliant, versed in ancient knowledge and contemporary science, and can create a better future for Roma and heal the wounds of our past.

Many of Drăgan's plays and short films, and her album *Tehno Vrăjitoarele* (*Techno Witches*) with Niko G, explore the Techno Witch and Roma Futurism. Drăgan has stated that while she does not identify as a witch, rituals and spells make up her performance art, and she collaborates with traditional Romani witches like the Minca family, who work as witches as part of their family trade and offer spells, rituals, and readings for clients. Drăgan hopes that by working with Romani witches and performing the art of witchcraft, their work will create true healing in that liminal space between art and magic.

The vision of the Techno Witch is not so far-fetched from where we're standing. Romani fortune-tellers and witches are expanding their businesses by using new technology. We meet with clients from all over the world with Zoom, and there are Romani witches streaming rituals on social media or televising ceremonies in documentaries or on YouTube. We're mastering SEO, algorithms, AI, and marketing strategies to hold our own as magical spaces become increasingly virtual. We're starting podcasts and other platforms not just to share what we do, but also to fight for our rights. Since Romani practices and archetypes are so popular in spiritual circles, why not take this opportunity to clarify who we are and center our true voices. Personally, the two of us love witches. We might even be them.

Our Vision for Romani Culture and Fortune-Telling

We see fortune-telling as an opportunity for us to share our cultural practices, raise awareness of the Romani people and the ongoing human rights crisis, humanize Romani people to non-Roma by creating good relationships with clients, and create more solidarity and support among Romani people from all over. Fortune-telling is a space for people who may or not fit in with their culture or society's parameters to safely seek spiritual guidance. And we also firmly believe that Roma of any gender can practice this or any trade or job they want.

It can be a tough line to walk between practicing our survival trade and playing into stereotypes to make a living, and we, the authors of this book, have not navigated this flawlessly, but we try our best. We are not trying to be picture-perfect Gypsies, and we're not trying to represent all of Romani culture, or even all Romani fortune-tellers. We are just ourselves, our imperfect, complex selves. We are writing this book to explore, honor, and uplift the history, practices, and perspectives of this Romani trade we love. We hope it opens the doors for more Romani people to share their perspectives.

We are not the last word on Romani fortune-telling either. Other Romani authors on divination and spirituality include April Wall, author of *Reading Tarot, Reading Tea Leaves*, and *Deciphering Angel Numbers*, Ylva Mara Radziszewski aka Bimbo Yaga, author of *A Practical Guide for Witches: Spells, Rituals, and Magic for an Enchanted Life*, and Lisa Boswell, author of *The Modern Oracle: Fortune Telling and Divination for the Real World*. We recommend these books so highly. While there are not a lot of books on divination published by Roma, there are far more books on "Gypsy Fortune-Telling" by non-Roma or people with varying connections to Romani heritage that are not particularly accurate and do a lot to reinforce stereotypes. We hope to see more true Romani authors with authentic, progressive information on the shelves in the future.

Romani Spirituality

Roma have a core of spiritual beliefs and cultural practices referred to as *Romanipen* (spellings vary) that reflect "Romani-ness" or what it is to be Romani, centering around physical and spiritual purity. Roma are also free to adopt a religion to practice alongside Romanipen, and over the centuries many have done this for personal and political reasons, and as a means of survival. There are Muslim, Catholic, Christian, Eastern Orthodox, Jewish, and Zoroastrian Roma—and more! It's easier, in theory, to be accepted by the dominant culture if you've adopted their religion. However, churches have had a history of not allowing Catholic and other Christian Roma to enter or be married inside.

This collection of spiritual and religious traditions unique to Roma in particular has given way to specific practices and deities. For instance, a goddess or saint, depending on your perspective, that many Roma share is Sara la Kali, whose name appears in other variations, including Kali Sara, Sara Kali, Saint Sarah, Black Sarah, or the Black Madonna. She was likely brought from India as the fierce Hindu goddess Kali, and she evolved over time, likely as Roma adapted to European life and custom. For more about this deity, refer to Ronald Lee's essay, "The Romani Goddess Kali Sara," which is easily found online. She is the protector of the Romani people, a divine mother figure with dark skin who looks like a peaceful Kali wearing the Madonna's robes who's traded in her skull necklace for flowers. She understands the world is wild and dangerous, and she does her best to protect us while respecting our free will. Many Roma tend to believe in a combination of free will and fate, which is reflected in our approach to fortune-telling, and life. Nothing is set in stone, and even the lines of your palm change over time, but certain events or paths may feel like destiny. We have to be tuned in to the world around us to survive and learn to dance with the Wheel of Fortune.

Sara la Kali

Illustration by Anna Rabko

CHAPTER 2

How to Strengthen
Your Intuition

Every culture has revered spiritual practices, and Roma are no exception. We are one of many ethnic groups who have used a spiritual trade not just for our own well-being, but also as a way to eke out a living and be successful among a dominant majority that could be hostile. Roma found allies with others and made themselves indispensable by offering an array of services and by sharing our culture. Both of us began our training for this work as children, and though we are not related, our families began with similar techniques. First, in our families, there was a recognition of ability, some display of intuition that marked us as ready to learn. Even if you didn't have this moment as a child, or no one noticed it, that doesn't mean that you don't have potential. Everyone has inherent intuition, and you can learn how to access it better and use it with purpose. Roma have a special relationship with intuition, but it might not be for the reasons you think.

Are Roma Really More Intuitive?

Romani people have been both celebrated and demonized for our intuitive powers. First, it's important for us to clear up that Roma are not any more inherently magical than any other ethnic group, and yet, we carry this reputation of the magical Gypsy that's both a blessing and a curse.

Our friend Pierce Horvath of Dead Scared Entertainment says "The ability is something you are born with. Every individual has this ability. I feel it is a matter of choice to channel and develop these gifts. It's like a muscle, needing regular stimulation and training to foster growth." We agree with Horvath, and we also feel that Roma do seem to have a fine-tuned sense of intuition, not necessarily more than other groups, but in the way that only systematically oppressed people do. Romani professor, editor, writer, and author of the memoir *American Gypsy*, Oksana Marafioti, explains why this is:

Reflecting on the history and cultural intricacies of the Romani people, our connection to mysticism emerges as a profound facet of our identity, and it unfolds against a backdrop of resilience amid centuries of adversity. We've endured a tumultuous history marked by discrimination, persecution, and marginalization. The collective memory of suffering within our community is deeply ingrained, a consequence of slavery, forced assimilation, and systemic violence.

Navigating a world often hostile to us, is it surprising that some Romani individuals appear to have developed a heightened sense of intuition? Could this intuitive capacity serve as an adaptive response, a survival mechanism cultivated through the psychological impact of our historical experiences? Similar to how an abused individual might become an empath and hyper-intuitive due to childhood trauma, is it possible that our community, as a whole, has evolved these heightened sensitivities for collective self-preservation?

I wonder if some of our cultural practices, including activities like fortune-telling and divination, extend beyond mere superstitions. Could these rituals be coping mechanisms developed over generations to decipher and comprehend the intentions of others?

I believe so. I believe the historical persecution endured by our community has necessitated an adeptness at reading social cues and predicting potential threats.

While outsiders may romanticize Romani intuition and spirituality, akin to how certain contemporary social media figures idealize empaths as uniquely attuned to the cosmic essence of nature, the reality is likely more nuanced. I recognize the authenticity of spiritual connections to the mystical. However, it's crucial to acknowledge that across generations, our heightened intuition and keen observational skills might also be reflective of the necessity for caution and self-preservation.

Jennileen Joseph, Ayurvedic naturopath, agrees that "as an extremely ostracized and marginalized people, Rroma have had to be very good at 'reading' others for survival. I think this has made us exceptionally good at divination practices because culturally it has become intuitive for many of us to read passive cues like body language, tone of voice, general affect." Jennileen, who also has a lineage of fortune-telling in her family, adds, "Given that Roma are from the same parts of India where healing practices like Ayurveda hail from, I notice we have integrated Ayurvedic diagnostic techniques such as what facial lines and nails mean in terms of a person's general constitution and therefore what physical and emotional issues a person may have because of those presenting physicalities. I think when we arrived in Europe, many of the intelligences we had coming from the East were seen as 'magic' and we never bothered to correct anyone about those things being actually based in science."

Roma of course have varying opinions on intuition, but we the authors believe that our intuition has helped our culture survive extremely hostile conditions, and Roma have learned to be on our toes and pay attention to everything, whether you come from a fortune-telling family or not. We would prefer that these skills didn't come from generations of trauma and oppression, but we also recognize that intuition and awareness are valuable. Unfortunately, the PTSD, anxiety, depression, illness, etc., that accompany trauma also make it difficult for survivors to continue surviving, which is why our personal practices of fortune-telling are centered in healing. We believe that teaching fortune-telling is beneficial to anyone whether you plan to be a professional reader or not, because intuition is a life skill that serves you everywhere, any time. It's a tough world out there. And we can't account for the trauma you already have, but our methods will probably not add any more trauma to your life. Our hope is that it's one of many methods that help you find some peace.

Paulina's Intuitive Training

Almost every woman in my family was a full-time fortune-teller. As soon as I could speak, I was expected to "tell fortune." That's what my family called it. As young as five, I remember the men in my family, usually uncles and grandfathers, letting me "'pretend'" to read their palms. We would sit on the couch, usually while the news was playing on TV, and they had their coffee out on the table. They would give me their palms and ask, "What can you tell me?" The women would laugh and even sometimes take pictures. They were laughing because I would usually repeat what I heard them say when they were giving readings. "You are going to be breaking up with someone you love dearly," and "Your life line is a little rough. Maybe some health issues?"

Thinking back, it was something I was just kind of expected to know, but those little moments were practice. I gained confidence and tried to be present and engaging. I was always taught that I needed to be captivating, with little details like eye contact and a stern voice. Once I knew how to play the part, they said the words would just come to me. The elders in the family, my aunts, and my mom would say, "When you are reading, you'll just get a feeling." I didn't really question it at all. Especially as a kid, I thought, "Okay, makes sense." I remember thinking that the feelings just come kind of like when I have the urge to pee. Out of nowhere, sometimes really strong, sometimes barely perceptible.

Just being taught that my intuition is a little thought or feeling at the forefront of my mind made me a better reader. I was told to take deep breaths and slow down if I was struggling. You can read all the manuals, take all the quizzes, and know the meaning of every card, but when you are sitting across from someone, you might feel nervous, forgetful, or distracted. My elders taught me if I was feeling nervous with a client, I should pretend my hardest, and fake it till I make it. Fake the feeling of being calm and confident. It worked for me, and maybe it will work for you.

Jezmina's Intuitive Training

The story goes that my grandmother knew I needed to be trained as a fortune-teller when, as a three-year-old, I toddled up to her while she was resting with her aching legs up in her comfy chair in front of the TV, while she was knitting away one afternoon, babysitting me in her trailer. My grandmother suffered from arthritis, and her knees were paining her badly that day. Though I didn't know about her suffering, I placed a hand on each of her knees and closed my eyes, keeping very still for about a minute. She said she felt my chubby hands grow hot like coals and they pulled the pain right from her body. I lifted my hands up triumphantly, and she said I drew back my arms and threw the pain out the window, and then marched away, laughing to myself. That's when she knew that I needed to be trained in the old family trade, and that my "fire hands" marked me as a healer.

Before my grandmother started teaching me tarot, palm, or tea-leaf reading, she taught me to meditate, though she did not call it that. I remember so clearly the day she started our training; I was about four years old. She led me into her bedroom in her trailer in Salem, New Hampshire, and we stood in front of the simple altar to her ancestors on top of her dresser that she prayed at every day. The dresser was painted white and affixed with a mirror, and the top of it she had covered with a lace doily and decorated with pictures of her family, glass crystals for the way they caught light to make rainbows, a crucifix, rosary, a bell with an angel on it, and a white tea light candle. She picked up the biggest glass crystal on the altar, a round teardrop shape the size of a crab apple, cut into many facets, and she told me that God is a beautiful, protective energy that is around us, and just like the faces of the crystal, God has many faces and names according to different people. She put the crystal in my hand and told me to imagine all of its rainbow-making sides were the many faces of the divine, and that this is whom I could connect with.

My grandmother taught me dream interpretation and meditation techniques to connect with this God energy, though she didn't call it meditation. We did these meditations often, every day I spent with her and before we practiced any divination. There were other little things we would do to ensure that I was guided and protected. She gave me a red thread with a bell attached to wear for protection around my neck. She made sure I was clean before we did spiritual work. We would at least wash our hands before we set to any fortune-telling lessons. We would pray to God for protection and guidance, and ask for our ancestors and for good spirits to guide us too. We would give thanks for our blessings, our lives, and our time together.

My grandmother also encouraged my natural connection to animals and plants. She believed the old animistic ways that everything has a spirit, and she taught me how to honor spirits by speaking with reverence and kindness to them, and making offerings of fruit, water, or prayers to nature if I was going to be in the woods. She taught me to listen to permission from nature, and the guardian spirits of nature, like asking permission to pick a dandelion and waiting to hear "yes" or "no" from it, and respecting the answer. She also taught me to get rid of bad spirits by firmly cursing them out. Reflecting on my childhood, I see that all of these moments with her were part of my intuitive training even before we started with cards, palms, and tea leaves.

The Importance of Protecting Yourself

In any spiritual tradition, there are rituals, practices, and charms for protection. Protective rituals make sure that your intuition doesn't suffer from interference, cloudiness, or anything else untoward. Ritual is important because it's grounding, reassuring, and helps create order in a chaotic world. The belief is that when people put energy behind rituals that have been carried on for generations, they grow in power. Whatever you believe is up to you, but we're sharing some beliefs and practices that we grew up with for you to try out and see how they feel for you.

What Is Energy?

There are so many ways to conceive of what energy is, and for the purposes of fortune-telling and our own spiritual perspective, we think energy can be emotions, thoughts, intentions, divinity, and more. It can be positive, negative, or neutral. Paulina likes to explain it like this: if you're sitting in a room of angry, messed-up people, you're going to leave that room feeling angry and messed up. Energy is empathy to some degree. Whether you're talking about the energy of universal love, or the bad vibes of the evil eye, it's the same thing. We work with energy, we protect against it, and we're responsible for the energy we put into the world.

Pto Pto an∂ Prikaӡa, Bibaxt an∂ Ba∂ Energɥ

The belief in luck (*baxt*) and bad luck (*bibaxt* or *prikaza*) is strong in our culture. Much like a belief in energy, what we say, do, think about, and even watch on TV all has energy, and some Roma can be superstitious, or perhaps just mindful, about all of it. Traditionally if you're talking about something unlucky, violent, or tragic, you would do something to protect yourself immediately afterwards, like pray, spit, make a religious sign, or something; otherwise the energy or bibaxt could linger and attach itself to you. For instance, when leaving a funeral, Paulina's family will pick up a handful of leaves from the cemetery, and as they are driving out the gates, throw the leaves backwards out the window and say *baxt ando kasht* (luck in the wood/luck in the tree) so the spirits attach themselves to the leaves instead of you. Fortune-tellers are especially cautious because you are dealing with both fortune and misfortune, and you want to make sure that your energy is clear as a bell while you're holding space for others, and not taking anyone's bibaxt home with you.

Our friends Pierce and Raquel Horvath, brother and sister duo, founded and run Dead Scared Entertainment, a Romani horror media company, and they produce *O Verda Darano* (The Wagon of Fear), which is a Romani storytelling podcast specializing in tales of horror and the supernatural. Pierce is an illustrator, animator, and a horror fan, while Raquel specializes in business and marketing, and she is also a petite fashion model.

For a lot of Roma, telling scary stories is one thing, as our culture has a long tradition of oral literature and folklore, but some Roma might make the sign of the cross, recite a prayer, burn a little frankincense, or ring some bells to chase away the bad energy. As far as watching horror movies, some Roma are superstitious and don't want those images in their homes. Pierce and Raquel laughed with us during our *Romanistan* and *O Verda Darano* podcast crossover episode when we discovered all of our families say "*pto pto*," like you're lightly spitting, whenever a bibaxt topic comes up in conversation or a horror movie comes on the TV to cast the energy away from you.

Pierce and Raquel are from a Catholic family and are practicing Catholics themselves, so many of their traditions reflect that. Pierce is a horror aficionado, and he says:

> I find that, even though it can be believed to open malevolent portals, scary movies don't scare or affect me energetically. Making horror films and being a fan changes the way I interact with the media, knowing that a great deal of what I'm watching is fabricated, even when based in fact. In general, I protect my energy in a rather traditional way. Being Catholic, I've fought literal demons through prayer and through meditating on O Del (God), Jesus Christ, The Blessed Virgin Mary, St. Michael, etc. I've been sensitive to energies, good and bad, from a young age so I find that I'm able to work with them more easily through the beliefs of the Catholic faith. Something as simple as blessing my space with Holy Water or saying a prayer while I shower and envisioning the washing off of bad energy does the trick.

Raquel doesn't like scary movies, though, and is a little nervous about them opening something up, or just tormenting her with anxiety, so when she's afraid, or if Pierce is making her watch a classic fright film, she says she's the first one to be crossing herself and saying all her prayers through the movie. If you're interested in horror films and race representation, listen to our season 1 *Romanistan* podcast episode "Horror Movies and Representation with Emani Jerome," one of our international-relations guests who is a BIPOC-focused educator, advocate, and ecosystem builder.

Bibaxt and bad energy can come in so many forms, and one of the most important ones is the evil eye. Many of the ways Roma protect themselves spiritually revolve around deflecting or avoiding this particularly dangerous energy.

The Evil Eye

The evil eye, also known as the *nazar, ayin hara, malocchio,* or *mal de ojo,* is a common and ancient belief across many cultures, spanning the world. Romani people call it *jakheli* (spellings vary), and the practice of removing it is called *jakhendar*, or even *jakhalipnasqo drabakăripen*. While practices and opinions vary among cultures, religions, and even Roma who believe in it, essentially it boils down to the belief that a glance can cause illness, harm, bad luck, or even death. Sometimes people cast the evil eye purposefully, or as a result of their envy or malice, and other times it can be totally accidental. Usually pregnant women, babies, and animals are the most vulnerable, but everyone is susceptible. Fortune-tellers need to be particularly careful too, because we are often dealing with people's energies, hopes, fears, and emotions, and because we need to protect ourselves and our livelihoods in the face of it.

In an age when people post their happiest moments on social media, or need to have a strong online presence to promote their businesses or otherwise flourish, it's smart to be protected practically, like security and data, and spiritually. As there are so many ways to become prey to the evil eye, there are many different ways to protect yourself. We are sharing some practices that are specifically Romani, but if you are not Romani, we encourage you to look into your family or cultural background and see what your people have historically done for protection. One book that we enjoyed was *Terrors of the Evil Eye Exposed* by Henri Gamache, which shares protection techniques from a number of countries and cultures, but there are others out there to explore.

Our families, and many others, are superstitious about sharing good news before its fruition in case anyone's envy disrupts the good luck and turns it into bad luck. It's important to be humble and not to brag about the good things in your life, not just because it's tacky to brag, but because it attracts the evil eye from others.

To protect from the evil eye, Raquel Horvath swears by "having something red on, wearing blessed holy medals, and some people even say to wear your underwear backwards. My trick is to just wear red undies." Jezmina's mom swore by red undies too. Raquel adds that, despite these tactics, "sometimes people's energy is just too strong, and none of the above works. Then, I like to bless myself with holy water and have my baba do jakhendar for me to get rid of it." Pierce agrees:

In public, one can wear a garment, usually their underwear or undershirt backwards, or have on something colored red to ward off these energies. Even a visible cross or evil eye pendant will do the trick. But, when the energy is much stronger than I can personally handle, I turn to our familial jakhendar practice. Jakhendar directly translates to "eye fall." We practice this ritual to remove the evil eye. Believe me, it is truly a literal removal at times. This practice varies from country to country and family to family. Our version involves the breaking of bread and a glass of water. It is up to a maternal figure, usually our Baba, to practice the ritual. It begins with the breaking of nine pieces of bread and dropping them in a glass of water. The more bread that falls, the stronger that evil energy on you is. And, after a series of crosses are signed on our forehead, throat, shoulders, and heart, the water and bread is thrown in the crook of the door between the frame of the house and where the hinges meet the panel. Skeptics and gadje may laugh, but it's practically cinematic how relieved and energized you feel once the ritual is complete.

Katelan Foisy, artist, designer, fortune-teller, and *Romanistan* podcast guest, shared a jakhendar ritual that she likes, and it's a popular one among Roma and similar to the bread ritual that the Horvaths do. All you need is a glass of fresh water that has never been drunk, your own spit, and nine matches. Katelan says, "Fill a cup with water. Spit into the cup three times. You do not have to spit large amounts. A spray will do. The way we make the sound pttthh [pto] will get enough of our spit/energy into the cup."

This is optional, but Katelan suggests that you can say the Lord's Prayer, or whatever other prayer you like, and then take a match and light it. Once it is lit, press the match head gently against the side of the cup until the head falls off. As you drop in the match heads, you say, "Not one, or two, or three, nor four, or five, or six, not even seven, eight, or nine." If the match head sinks to the bottom of the cup, then the evil eye is on you. Katelan suggests that you do this ritual in groups of three, so nine times in all with nine matches. If the match heads keep sinking to the bottom of the cup, then that represents how many people cast the evil eye on you. So if three match heads fall to the bottom, it means three people have the evil eye on you. Katelan explains:

> If you have the evil eye on you, then you need to take a sip of your coal or match water. The term coal water is used because originally it was pieces of coal thrown into water. Or at least that is what I've heard. I've only ever done this with matches. Then you dip your fingers into the water and make the sign of the cross onto your being. You can also wash yourself down with the water. The coal or matches dispel the evil eye and cleanse you. The way people dispose of this is different. I drink the water and use the rest to place onto my hands and wash myself off. I've heard of other ways of disposing of it as well, like throwing it out the door.

This is a simple and powerful ritual to gauge the evil eye and rid yourself of it in a pinch. If making the sign of the cross conflicts with your beliefs, you can make any protective sign you want, or just dab yourself three times with the water. You can listen to our interview with Katelan in season 3, and she also has a blog on her website *katelanfoisy.com* if you want more art and magical lifestyle content from her.

Cleansing and Protecting Your Space

So much of Romani spirituality hinges on cleanliness, which makes sense because with a long history of slavery, persecution, and extreme poverty, Roma did not always have access to sanitation (and many still don't) so cleanliness is literally life or death. There are strong binaries within the culture, particularly what is considered clean or unclean, or what is Romani and what is gadje (non-Romani). The book *We Are the Romani People*, by Dr. Ian Hancock, goes into detail on what is considered *marime*, or unclean, if you would like to know more.

As two rebel spirits, we tend to challenge traditions that feel outdated to us. For instance, the belief that the menstrual cycle is unclean feels neither true nor helpful to us, though we understand why the belief exists. It seems to feed into the sexist belief that women are less than men. We're still going to wash our clothes and our bodies well and regularly, no matter the time of the month, but, personally, we're losing the stigma that comes with being born into a female body. And, while we're here talking about gender, we're recognizing that gender identity is highly personal and self-determined and absolutely transcends biological sex, and biological sex is much more nuanced than many realize anyway. However, other practices around cleanliness and spirituality, like the ones we're sharing, feel good to us. We love the idea of the home as a pure and sacred place where we rest, play, cook, and spend time with people who matter most to us, including ourselves. Protecting and caring for our space help create a place where we can do spiritual work safely and with clarity. It makes sense to us to cleanse before and after spiritual work.

There is not a lot of distinction between physical and spiritual purity—the two overlap quite a lot. Sweeping, vacuuming, and mopping your home daily keep the floors sparkling, sure, but they also keep out bad energy, like bad luck, unhappy spirits, illness, depression, or any other unwanted energy. Envision that as you clean the space, you are also cleansing the energy and clearing room for blessings and abundance. While cleaning, many Roma will also burn frankincense to further purify and cleanse, or an incense that incorporates it. Jezmina's mom loved to burn Nag Champa. It's a good idea to open a window for a little while as you do this to let the stale energy out. If business is slow and money isn't coming into the house, Paulina's family likes to mix up a pot of salt and hot soapy water, and then throw the potion out the door to change the luck and bring money back in. However, when you're cleaning, don't ever sweep out the front door because that sweeps out all your luck. And there's no cleaning or sweeping on New Year's Day, even if you had a big party the night before, because you'll be cleaning away all your luck for the year otherwise. This is a hard rule for Roma to follow because most of us are clean freaks.

In general, a cluttered space can distract the mind, so doing your best to keep your home clean and tidy is the, perhaps surprising, first step to strengthening your intuition. It can be tough to keep up with everything, so just do your best. No one is asking for perfection. If you have family living with you, try to encourage everyone to pitch in, even little ones, and make cleaning as positive as possible by playing great music, using cleaning products that smell good (if you can tolerate scents), and giving out lots of compliments for everyone's hard work, including your own.

Many Romani families hang bells on the doorknobs and sometimes even the windows to protect the space from bad energy or mischievous spirits. The ringing clears the space and chases naughty spirits away. Even if families don't hang bells, it's common practice to tie a red ribbon around the front doorknob from inside the home. Red is a very protective, lucky color and is used a lot in protective charms.

Cleansing and Protecting Yourself

We love a good hot shower with scrubbing and soap, or a nice thorough handwashing. This is true for the mundane reasons of keeping clean, and for spiritual purposes. Before doing any kind of important spiritual work, it's common practice to cleanse yourself in some way, like washing your face, hands, or whole body. This is especially true if you feel sick, tired, depressed, or angry, or if you're just having a bad day. You can't really wash all your problems away, but the idea is that you can at least energetically shift some of the discomfort, or wash away the prikaza, or the bad luck. For this reason, it's also good practice to cleanse yourself after a shift of giving readings for people, or after any heavy or stressful interaction. The most important part is strongly visualizing or imagining that, as you bathe, you are washing away any negative energy. Imagine that the products you use to bathe, whether they're just a soap you like or something more magical, are also protecting you as you go on with your day. We love soap from Romani creators Luludi and Kushan Creations.

You can also protect yourself by washing your hair, especially in rainwater, but any water will do. If the prikaza feels particularly bad, you can even cut or trim your hair. It doesn't have to be a dramatic, post-breakup style "I'm getting bangs now" kind of haircut, though it can be, but trimming away the old makes room for the new. If your hair is long enough, and you feel like there is bad luck or bad vibes around, braid that hair, and if you can weave in red ribbons for added protection, even better. If braiding and ribbons don't feel right to you, but you still want to try this, you could use red hair ties, clips, headbands, a red hat, or a hat with a red accent.

Upon entering your home after spending time out in the world, many Roma take off their shoes, change their clothes, and wash their hands or even shower before settling in. Practically, you are making sure you're not carrying more germs than necessary inside your home, but there's also the benefit of ridding yourself of any unwanted energies that might be trying to hitch a ride with you. Changing into your "house clothes" can be so comforting, too, and it signals to your brain that you're in your safe space. Almost all of our magical practices have practical applications too.

Types of Intuition

Sometimes people think they are not intuitive because they don't understand how their intuition works. Everyone has their gifts, specialties, and ways of sensing. Here are some common types of intuition.

Clairvoyance: seeing, which can manifest as seeing images inside your mind and/or seeing energy, spirits, auras, etc. in the world around you.

Clairsentience: feeling, which can be deep empathy, or the ability to feel the emotions or energy of people, animals, plants, the environment, and more. You might be able to feel illness or pain in others.

Claircognizance: knowing, which means you might have intuitive information come to you as thoughts, or have psychic precognizance, just knowing that something will happen before it happens.

Clairaudience: hearing, which could be voices of spirits, guides, deities, ancestors, plants, animals, etc. that sound either from inside your mind or outside of it.

Clairalience: smelling, which is a rarer one, but some people show intuitive ability through scent, like smelling an ancestor's pipe smoke when they come to pay you a visit from beyond or leave you a message. Many Roma believe that smelling frankincense means that your departed loved ones are visiting you.

Clairgustance: tasting, which is the rarest, but sometimes people will have certain tastes in their mouths that appear to communicate psychic information, like the taste of a client's grandma's favorite cookies, or the taste of blood when detecting danger.

Pay Attention

Pay close attention to how you receive information. Do you get a clairsentient pit in your stomach when someone seems sketchy to you? Or do you have a claircognizant knowing? Do you hear a little clairaudient voice giving you good advice in your head? Meditation and grounding practices can help you be aware and receptive enough to learn how your psychic senses work, and that attention will help you develop them, and maybe even expand into new senses.

During a reading, one of Jezmina's clients was expressing concern that she talks to her patron goddess all the time, but she feels like the goddess doesn't talk back to her. Then a moment later, this client noted that a phrase that Jezmina said in the reading, "to leave offerings in honor of your past self's resilience," was strange because she kept hearing a similar phrase in her head over the past few weeks that felt important and seemed to come from nowhere. "That's her!" Jezmina said. "That's your goddess!" Jezmina thinks that turn of phrase came to mind in the reading to show the client that her flashes of claircognizance are sometimes messages from her deities and spirits. Sometimes readings confirm your own psychic experiences.

Even if the signs and communication that come to you are subtle, you can begin to notice what seems like it's coming from you, and what's coming from "nowhere," which could actually be from a guide, angel, ancestor, deity, your higher self, the universe, plants, elements . . . or whatever you connect with.

Intuitive Exercises

These are some exercises that we grew up with and continue to use, and it is the practice that makes them powerful. You can always tailor these exercises to suit your own needs. The most important thing is that you find a way to make them work for you.

Clearing Clouds

This simple meditation is a beautiful and succinct way to purify your energy and open yourself to your own intuitive wisdom or to divine guidance. Jezmina's grandmother taught this simple meditation to teach little Jez how to keep a clear mind and open up the third eye. The way grandma saw it, doing a meditation like this sweeps away your thoughts so you can open your mind to the divine. Whether you believe your intuition comes from gods, goddesses, spirit guides, the universe, nature, your higher self, or anywhere else, this meditation can work. The trick is to do it consistently. It's the practice that makes it powerful.

- Take full deep breaths and imagine your mind is a beautiful blue sky spotted with clouds
- As you breathe, understand that those clouds represent thoughts
- Let your steady, deep breath blow the cloud-thoughts away
- As the sky clears, your mind clears and is open to messages
- Do this every day, before readings, during readings if you feel clouded, and any time you need to open your intuition

Candle Gazing

The first, and perhaps the most important intuitive practice is fire gazing, which eventually evolves into the more advanced practice of fire and smoke reading. Early Roma lived on the road and often camped, and some still do, though camping rights for Gypsies, Roma, and Travellers are constantly threatened and taken away, creating dangerous or impossible living conditions for nomadic people. The campfire was the place where people would gather to cook, eat, tell stories, share gossip, make plans, sing, dance, and bond. Whether it was an evening of joy or sorrow, it took place around the fire.

The campfire features in the extraordinary novel *The Color of Smoke* by Romani writer Menyhért Lakatos, which is the first major novel that chronicles the lives of Eastern Europe's Roma. In the story, the main character's grandmother sees a shape in the campfire smoke that foretells evil ahead, and this is the foreshadowing for World War II and the Nazi regime that sent so many Romani people, including the main character's family, to death camps, or to chaotic executions in the forest. It is a chilling and solemn moment, and everyone understands they need to take the omen seriously, even if there is little hope for survival. This example, though from Romani literature, shows how real Romani intuition has had to be. Our history is rich, but it's also dark, violence-soaked, and painful. Some decisions were life and death. When people are consistently in danger, spirituality can become a tool for survival alongside all our expected, practical tools of evasion, combat, and empowerment.

Fire gazing is a beautiful, primal practice that people from all ethnic groups, including Roma, have likely been practicing since the beginning of human existence, and you can draw on your own roots to personalize your practice. To try fire gazing, you need only basic tools. Traditionally, of course, you would use a campfire, perhaps in a stone pit. Not everyone has access to that, so if you're working with a candle in your bedroom, that's absolutely okay. In the Hatha Yoga tradition, which originated in India, candle flame gazing meditation, or *trataka sadhana* in Sanskrit, is meant to strengthen the third eye, the seat of our psychic ability. Both of us practice yoga, not because it's a Romani tradition (it isn't), but because we love it and it helps us feel connected to our culture's distant Indian roots. Romani linguists and language experts, such as Ronald Lee, Dr. Ian Hancock, Dr. Hristo Kyuchukov, and Erik Decker, show how even the Romani language is still significantly influenced by its Sanskrit roots. We wonder if, as part of the Indian diaspora, we carry on other practices and traditions like fire gazing, but with our own twist.

Fire gazing was Jezmina's mother's favorite practice, and she encouraged little Jez to stare into the candle flame, the campfire, and the woodstove to develop their nascent psychic ability. To start candle gazing, you can use any kind of candle and light it any way you want to. In the yogic tradition, you would do this meditation in the early morning when it is still dark out, but we believe that doing things imperfectly is better than not doing them at all, so if you know you're the type of person who's never going to meditate at dawn, that's fine. Do it whenever you can. It's always nice to use a candle that's ethically made of eco-friendly ingredients, but whatever you have on hand will do, just as long as it's in a firesafe dish or holder. Set the candle a couple of feet away from you and sit comfortably. In this meditation, you will focus both on your breath and on the candle flame before you. Keep your breath as deep and as steady as your gaze.

In traditional trataka meditation, you are meant to keep your eyes open as long as possible as you gaze at the flame, and when you finally close them, try not to rub away any tears. Let the tears refresh your eyes, and as your eyes are closed, continue to imagine the candle before you in your mind's eye. If you don't like this part of the practice, you can just focus on the candle and blink naturally, and still gain tremendous benefits. As you are fire gazing, keep your thoughts focused on the flame as well. You might even imagine the flame purifying and opening your third eye, warming you with psychic blessings. Try this practice for five minutes daily, and over time, you can build up to fifteen minutes a day. Consider too that everything has a spirit, objects, plants, animals, elements, everything, including fire, and by sitting with a flame every morning, you are building a relationship with the element of fire. As you strengthen this relationship by showing up regularly to spend time with the flame, you will begin to learn how fire communicates.

Then you have the option to evolve this candle meditation into fire reading, which we will cover in Chapter 7: Advanced fortune-telling Techniques.

How to Sense People's Energy

Whether you are reading someone's fortune or just reading the vibe in a room, sensing people's energy is a crucial skill. It can fill in the gaps in a reading and help you personalize whatever the tarot cards, palms, or tea leaves say. Reading energy can help you in any other situation too— it's so helpful to be able to intuit if someone is being genuine or has self-serving intentions, for instance. Reading the vibe of a potential landlord, date, loan officer, salesperson, employer, or client are all incredibly valuable. We tend to approach energy reading through these points: body language, empathy, eye contact, and touch.

Body Language

There are plenty of books on reading body language, and because of cultural differences, neurodivergence, and other factors, it's not a universally applicable science, so we don't want to pretend to be experts in anything we're not. However, we encourage you to notice body language, if someone seems to be standing too close or too far, if they seem hunched and nervous, or tall and confident. Pay attention to the body language of people you observe out in the world, and the feelings you associate with it. It's that last part, the feelings you have that are sparked by someone's mannerism or way of being, that really matters. Try to suspend your judgment about what you think about what someone is or isn't doing with their body, and instead focus on how their body language feels to you.

Empathy

If you are naturally an empath then you know that when someone is upset, the feeling is almost palpable. You sense their sadness in the air, or even in your own heart. A good reader knows how to use that skill to gain more insight into the person and their present, as well as their past and future. The divinatory tools we use help us do this, but empathy is the key to unlocking those doors. Reading a person's energy is deeply linked to your ability to feel empathy for others. Once you begin to feel real compassion and empathy for a person, you are more connected to them, and your intuition heightens. On a more practical level, when we care about how someone feels and can imagine what that must be like, we understand them and their situation better. So as soon as a person sits down with you for a reading, center yourself with the cloud meditation or your own version of it, and then conjure up feelings of empathy. We often do this when we ask the person what brings them to us today, if they have any questions or intentions they would like to focus on, or if they just want to be open to anything. Whether they spill their guts about a problem that's bothering them, or say they need direction in their career, or just tell you, "I think I'll just see what comes up today," take a moment and really feel the request, and care about their perspective.

We both find it more difficult to read for people whom we don't like, or who rub us the wrong way, or act defensive, rude, or suspicious. At times like this, it's more apparent than ever that empathy is linked to intuition. We have to dig down deep to find our empathy and compassion for the person who irks us and who might be sitting across from our reading table and see them as just another person who feels pain and who has dreams and is just trying to make it in this chaotic world, even if they're, for whatever reason, a very off-putting presence at that moment. The Vietnamese Buddhist monk, Thich Nhat Hanh, taught loving-kindness meditations in which you wish another person and eventually the whole world to be well, happy, peaceful, healthy, safe, and so on. It's one of many beautiful exercises in many spiritual traditions that foster compassion for all. We highly recommend practicing wishing others well, even those people whom you're not so fond of. It's easier to wish people well when you recognize that when people are well, they have a chance to be their best selves, to be more self-aware, to change for the better, and to wish others well in turn.

Empathy Exercise

Before you go to bed, or right when you wake up, take a few minutes to send loving-kindness and compassion to yourself. Perhaps place your hands over your heart, and truly wish yourself well, wish yourself happiness, forgiveness, joy, safety, understanding, freedom, and everything good you can think of. Even if you feel like you're faking it, do your best impression of self-love. It will get easier the more you practice. Then choose someone who is on your mind, and send those loving-kindness wishes to them. Then think of someone whom you're not so fond of and send loving-kindness to them too. You don't need to choose anyone who has deeply hurt you, unless you think it would be helpful for you. It's okay to just choose the stranger who cut you off on the way to work. Be as genuine as you can as you wish them well. Send this love to your town, your country, your continent, and then the whole world, and then the universe. Pour love out through your heart, because love is endless, and love connects you harmoniously to everything. If you do this regularly, ideally every day, it will be much easier to call up some empathy on demand when you need it, whether you're in a reading or diplomatically navigating a challenging moment with a difficult person.

Eye Contact

Natural yet consistent eye contact during a reading helps you tune in to the client's emotional and spiritual energy and show that you care about and understand their thoughts and concerns. If you like making eye contact, it can evoke a sense of trust and openness, and act as a bridge further connecting you, enabling you to interpret the subtle cues that transcend verbal communication. However, some people dislike eye contact and find it stressful, and that is absolutely valid and something to be mindful of. If your client is avoiding eye contact, don't force it. And if you don't like it, then you don't need to force it either. It's more important that everyone feels safe and comfortable. We'll discuss tips for navigating this during a reading in Chapter 10: How to Be Convincing.

Eye Contact Exercise

If you're okay with eye contact, it can be helpful to practice intuitive eye contact with a loved one, friend, or even a friendly stranger whom you'd like to get to know better, and who is also into eye contact. Consent is key. When everyone is comfy, these exercises work much better. To practice intuitive eye contact, all you need to do is sit across from the person who's practicing with you, clear your mind with a meditation, set a timer for one minute, and stare into each other's eyes. You are allowed to blink. While you are holding the other person's gaze, try to keep the sky of your mind clear of clouds, and just focus on their eyes. The gaze unlocks your psychic senses, so remain open to the thoughts, feelings, visions, sounds, and even scents and tastes that arise in this minute. When the timer chimes, share your experiences with each other and see what you picked up from each other. Even if you had a seemingly "random" vision, like a brown puppy playing on the beach, share it anyway. Those are usually the best ones because they are so specific. Maybe your partner is wishing to get a new canine companion and take them on an adventure. You won't know unless you share, and the more you share, the more you learn.

Try to practice this exercise more than once, and with different people, and try increasing the time from one minute to two, and up to five minutes.

Touch

Touch with consent is a great way to get a feel for a person, literally and psychically. When done safely, it fosters trust and emotional intimacy, and can activate the release of oxytocin, often referred to as the "bonding hormone." When a practitioner incorporates touch, such as holding a client's hand during a palm reading, it directly communicates empathy, support, and a shared presence without speaking a word. Moreover, touch can enhance the practitioner's ability to read the client and can offer valuable insights into their emotional state and energy. If you know you tend to be clairvoyant or visionary, paying special attention to how the palm looks as a whole will be essential for you, but beyond that, you might close your eyes while you hold the person's hand for a moment and see what is conjured up in your mind's eye. If you know that you are more clairsentient, focus on the feeling of their hand and notice what emotions arise in you in different parts of their palm.

However, consent is key. With consent, touch has the potential to alleviate tension and create a safe space, encouraging the client to open up more freely about their thoughts and concerns. Ask if the client is okay with you holding their hand during a palm reading. Tell them they can move around, readjust, or take a break whenever they want if they need to. If you practice hands-on healing of any kind, always ask if touch is okay, and remind them that they can give you feedback about pressure, stopping, or anything else. Even if they consent to touch, still let people know when and where you're going to touch them too so it's not a surprise.

Touch Exercise

If you can practice on a loved one, friend, or even a friendly stranger, all the better. Ask if you can hold their hand, then take some deep breaths and imagine all of your senses opening. You might like to practice the cloud meditation to start. Set a timer for three minutes, and as you hold their hand in yours, notice what it physically feels like. Is their hand cool or warm? Is their skin rough or smooth? Muscular, fleshy, or bony? What does all of that mean to you? If it's okay with your partner, get a good feel of their entire hand, their fingers, nails, and trace the lines of their palms. Which of your five senses are most activated? This is like psychic first impressions. Try closing your eyes, and opening them, and see if that makes it easier or harder to sense, or if it changes the type of information you get. Be open to any thoughts, emotions, visions, sounds, scents, or tastes that arise, and when the three minutes are up, share what came up for you.

Remember to share even the seemingly random bits of sensory data or thoughts. That's how you improve your accuracy. Try to practice this exercise more than once, and with different people, and let your partner take a turn too if they want to. It's always good to learn with others because you will learn from each other too.

Developing Your Own Psychic Lexicon

Everyone has their own omens, signs, and symbols. You all have your special ways of sensing and knowing. You have your guides, ancestors, and your unique set of beliefs and ways of seeing the world. One of the most helpful things you can do for yourself is keep some kind of journal or record of your psychic development. We especially recommend that you keep a dream journal, too. Dream interpretation was a big part of both of our training, and it's a less common skill that we offer to clients. In the US, folks say that talking about your dreams is boring, but we take dreams very seriously.

CHAPTER 3

Dream Divination

Dream divination is the cornerstone of fortune-telling for both of our families, and many others. Dreams are a liminal space, between worlds, where ancestors, spirits, messages, and symbols can reach you. Dreams are also a place where the subconscious throws its deepest concerns onto a screen for you to watch and sift through. Repressed emotions are never good for our well-being. For that reason, Western psychology is preoccupied with dream interpretation, with Jung being the most recognizable name in dream interpretation, and much of his practice draws from much older wisdom and symbols from other cultures, mainly from what is broadly considered the East. For that reason, some of our approach to dream analysis may be familiar already, because our culture and many others were inspiration for a differently packaged Western approach. At the same time, we all have personal experiences with symbols, perhaps in ways that are very different from the cultures we come from.

Ultimately, knowing and caring for yourself keep you grounded enough to be a good reader. We have years of experience delving into dreams, and while we refer to our shared cultural background, we created this chapter in a way that anyone can use our techniques for navigating the world of dreams.

Jezmina's Story

My grandmother was taught by her grandparents that dreams are how we expand and understand our intuition, and communicate with ancestors and divinity. She understood dream interpretation to be foundational to any divinatory practice. I often slept over at my grandmother's trailer, and a regular part of my training was discussing our dreams every morning. She was teaching me to interpret dreams bit by bit, by helping me understand my own, but also sharing some of hers with me. Around the same time she began teaching me dream interpretation, when I was about four, my grandfather, her ex-husband, died by suicide. He was a very violent and troubled man, an American WWII veteran who plucked my grandmother out of the postwar wreckage of Germany when she was just nineteen, and he left lifetimes of trauma in his wake.

The only dream my grandmother had back then was the same scenario on repeat: she dreamed that she was running, and that my mother and her siblings were children again, and they were running with her. In the dream, my grandfather chased them aiming his rifle with a wild look in his eyes, something that had happened before in the waking world. The scene would change from dream to dream—sometimes they were at home, in a store, or in a forest. The dream always ended the same way. My grandmother would find somewhere to hide her children, a closet, a cave, a tucked away place, and sigh with relief that they were safe. Then she would face my grandfather, and he would fill her with bullets until she woke up. Hearing this dream over and over when we woke in the mornings, sun streaming into the bedroom, wrapped up in her big German feather down covers, taught me at a very young age that many of the dreams we have are not about us navigating the future, but rather, surviving the past.

Paulina's Story

Growing up, my family believed anyone who knew us who had passed on would be able to reach us through our dreams. I was taught our dreams were a portal to communicate with our loved ones and see how their spirits were doing. For example, if they asked for food in our dream, we couldn't give it to them. Hungry spirits meant that they were unsettled in the after-life, and if we gave them food, we could be prolonging their suffering, because they needed to accept that they are not in this world anymore.

Many dream interpretations that I was raised with meant the opposite of what they seemed. How could dreaming of money and abundance mean coming into problems with business in the real world? This baffled me as a kid, but after reading many books from our family store collection and badgering my great-grandparents, I learned about the aspect of psychology behind dreams. Little things made sense. Dreaming of money in any way meant even your subconscious was too concerned about money, and this couldn't be good for you moving forward. Maybe all the superstitions had some scientific roots. Now I see many articles and books around the psychology behind our dreams and I believe this strongly intersects with Romani dream divination, where we can find similarities with many other cultures around the world.

Prophetic Dreams

Even so-called prophetic dreams, or dreams that predict the future, are rarely straightforward. For many people, even very intuitive people, prophetic dreams can be relatively rare, usually appearing in times of crisis, or more confusingly, in flashes of deja vu that don't seem important at all. We've met some people who dream in prophecy every night, but if that's not your reality, you're not alone. Luckily, most of our day-to-day life is made up of small events, not crises, and doesn't warrant dramatic dream intervention. The small events are important, though, and they take up a lot of our time and emotional energy. Most dreams are like this too, reflections and fragments of our smaller concerns, or the background noise of our deeper issues, burbling up from the subconscious. The idea is that if we can use these "mundane" dreams as helpful tools to understand ourselves and our lives, the bigger, more profound dreams will be easier to spot and understand too.

There might be times when you do get a warning in a dream and you really feel it in your bones or your gut. It's wise to listen to that. You might have already experienced this, and typically it's something you feel in your whole body. This has happened to us too—it's important not to assume that every bad dream is a warning, though. There are probably indicators that help you know when a dream truly is a warning, like certain people or guides delivering the message in an unmistakably clear way.

Some common symbols in prophetic dreams for Roma vary. Sometimes what we dream actually means the opposite. Like if you dream of a relative giving birth to a baby boy, it might actually be a girl. Many Roma believe hair and teeth falling out in a dream represents your troubles or worries leaving your life, so it's actually a good dream. Seeing a little blood in a dream means good luck, but seeing a lot of blood means bad luck. Seeing money means it will come your way, but touching money in the dream is bad because your subconscious might be too greedy or worried about money. Touching money can even mean there are rumors or negative words circulating in your life. Dreaming about cash in general may be a particularly Romani experience because for almost our whole existence, we worked with only cash, and many still do. Many Roma weren't even allowed to open bank accounts, and in some places that's still true. Present day, some families still don't trust banks or the government with their money at all because of that history. Most people get paid through their bank accounts or paychecks, and some businesses do take cash only, but in a Roma family, your whole lineage dealt only with cash, so physical money, such as dollars and coins, is very significant to us.

Animals in Dreams as Prophecy

Romani culture, like all other cultures, tends to have certain associations with animals and plants. And then certain Romani subgroups, or vitsas, might have their own associations, and families their own, and individuals as well. It can get very personal and specific, and not everyone agrees all the time on what certain animals mean. You might find this yourself—maybe you love an animal that many tend to shun, like spiders, and maybe an animal that most tend to love, like dogs, makes you uncomfortable. Take all of this into account when you're interpreting your dreams.

When we first started collaborating on *Romanistan* podcast together, we realized that both of our families believed dreaming about animals signaled either a prophetic dream, or a prophetic aspect of a dream. For instance, both of our families tend to read birds as bearers of news, whether it's good or bad. In Paulina's family, snakes represent gossip, and in Jezmina's, snakes represent change. Fish represent fertility, abundance, and manifestation in both of our traditions. In Paulina's family, dogs represent spirits or ancestors visiting you, and in Jezmina's, dogs represent protection or a loyal and faithful friend. These are just a few of many examples, but the trick is to learn what these animals represent for you specifically.

Examples of Prophetic Dreams

It can be helpful to have examples so you know how prophetic dreams work for others, even if you have your own experiences. Intuition can expand and evolve over time, so there's always plenty to learn. We will share a couple of prophetic dreams from our own lives with the lessons we learned from them.

Jezmina's Prophetic Dream

When I was in my first year at college, I had a brand new roommate, Sarah, whom I was already very fond of even though we had known each other only a couple of weeks. She was an adorable music-blaring, tennis-playing punk in a dog collar, denim dress, and red Chucks, and I knew we were going to be great friends, and we still are to this day. I don't sleep well, so I wake up pretty frequently. As such, I have a strong distinction between night dreams and morning dreams, and I've noticed that most of my spiritual healing or processing dreams come at night and most of my prophetic dreams come in the early morning. One morning, I dreamed that Sarah was driving her car at the time, a sporty red '93 Subaru SVX that she called "Back to the Future" because it looked like the DeLorean. In the dream, I was like a spirit hovering over her shoulder, and I saw the lights on her dashboard all light up like a Christmas tree, the car start to shake, and Sarah try to hit the brakes, but they wouldn't work, and she veered off the road and got into a terrible wreck.

I woke up gasping, and both of our alarms were going off. I felt fear jangling through my body, and I had a very clear message for her that seemed to come from the dream, and not my brain. "Sarah, you have to get your car checked out. You can't drive more than a mile, so go to the place next to the school on Williamson Road. Your brakes are almost gone and they won't make it any further than that."

"What are you talking about?" she said, sitting up in her bed and rubbing her eyes.

"Listen, I know it's weird, but I get messages in my dreams sometimes, and I just had one, and I just know you'll get in an accident if you don't take care of this today, right now. Trust me."

Sarah looked at me in silence for a little while. I thought for sure I had scared her off. I hadn't explained my fortune-telling or anything about myself that would give this more context. Witchy behavior wasn't that cool or trendy back in 2004 like it is now. I was bullied for being different as a kid, and I was worried that my new friend would think I was spooky too. But then she nodded her head and said, "Okay. If it'll make you feel better, I'll do it right now."

"Thank you!" I said. "It would make me feel better."

So she left right away and brought Back to the Future to the nearest auto shop. Later that morning, I ran into Sarah in the hallway of the English building.

"You were right!" she yelled, raising her arms and clenching her hands into celebratory fists. Everyone in the hallway turned to see what the commotion was all about. "My brakes were just about to go! The guy at the shop said it was a miracle I made there in one piece. *Damn*, you're good!"

After that, Sarah told this story to all of her friends, and news of my intuition spread far and wide. It ended up being great for my little fortune-telling side hustle, and she was my biggest supporter. I was just glad she and Back to the Future were safe and sound.

Paulina's Prophetic Dreams

Why are we so good at predicting car accidents? When I dream of swimming through water, that tends to be a warning that I'm going to get into a car accident. I was taught by my family that dreaming of water at all was usually a bad omen. Recently, I had a feeling that something was going to happen to my car when I dreamed that a tsunami had swept over my town. After that dream, I noticed that little things around me, electronics and the like, stopped working or even began falling apart. I am so used to this kind of warning in my dream that I decided to preemptively trade my car in, and on the way home with the new one, someone rear-ended me. I felt like I couldn't escape my fate no matter how hard I tried. It wasn't a serious accident, but why did I need to get into an accident at all? Was I projecting? Could it have been worse? I learned that I should trust my instincts but accept my fate at the same time. I believe we should take precautions for sure, and our intuition pushes us out of our comfort zone and challenges us in ways we wouldn't have imagined.

Sleep Quality

Quality of sleep is helpful, though not necessary, for dreamwork. Both of us have struggled with insomnia, nightmares, and night terrors since we were kids, but we have still been able to gain a lot of insight from dreams. Some people sleep well with very little effort, and some of us need to put some work into it. Even if you can't relate to the struggle to sleep, these tips and tricks for a better night's rest can still be very helpful.

Data-Driven Sleep Tips

Have a set bedtime every night. If you lose track of time, you can set bedtime alarms. Try setting one for when you want to start getting ready for bed, and another for when it's time to go to sleep.

Most people sleep better in dark rooms. Investing in blackout curtains might help.

Some people need quiet, while others sleep best with sounds, like rain, white noise, soft music, or even podcasts. Experiment with what works best for you. Set a sleep timer for music or a podcast so it doesn't play sound all night and wake you up later. Avoid falling asleep to the TV if possible because it casts disruptive light.

Find the room temperature that's ideal for you. Studies show that many people sleep best at slightly cooler temperatures, but that's not necessarily true for everyone. Experiment.

Avoid eating and drinking two hours before bed. It's okay to have a little water or non-caffeinated herbal tea if you take medication or supplements before bedtime.

Try to stay off your electronics a couple of hours before bed. If you need an activity to unwind, opt for reading, drawing, knitting, etc.

Exercise earlier in the day. Studies show that daytime physical activity helps people sleep better at night.

If you get a little snacky after dinner or prefer something light instead of a full evening meal, these foods have been shown to promote a good night's sleep. Having a small snack two hours before bed is totally fine for most people, unless you find that doesn't work for you. Everyone is different, so listen to your body.

- A cup (8 oz.) of tart cherry juice
- A kiwi
- A handful of almonds
- A handful of walnuts
- A banana

... maybe combine these for a smoothie?

People also tend to sleep better in clean, tidy, pleasant-smelling bedrooms. Cool and neutral colors are popular in bedrooms because they tend to be relaxing. Lighting, scent, and sound can be very helpful for signaling to your brain that it's time to unwind.

Bedtime Ritual: Romani Style

Our best bedtime rituals that we can share for protected and spiritually nourishing sleep are all about cleanliness, as you might expect.

Wash your sheets regularly and use linen sprays to purify and refresh.

Try not to wear your street clothes inside, and definitely don't sleep in them.

Keep your bedroom tidy, swept, vacuumed, and mopped.

Ideally, shower before bed, but at least wash your face and hands, and brush your teeth.

If you have long hair, you can braid it before bed to protect yourself from bad dreams or spirits. Extra points if you use red ribbons or hair ties.

Keep an evil-eye bead or other protective charm near where you sleep, and if you're having nightmares, you can tie a red ribbon around your wrist or ankle.

As you are cleansing your body and space, imagine washing away everything that no longer serves you and calling in pure, good energy and blessings.

Bedtime Bath for Good Dreams

There's an old cultural aversion to bathing in still water, so some Roma prefer showers to baths, but a lot of Roma people, if they take baths, will take a shower before and after, and always wash the tub with a good cleanser. For the bath, we suggest warm water or your preferred temperature.

Light candles (blue, purple, green, pink, or white) and incense if you like. When lighting, ask for protection and guidance from your guides, deities, ancestors, wise self, etc.

For the bath:

- ½ cup to 2 cups of Epsom salts

- Optional few drops of flower water, like rose, lavender, chamomile, Florida water, or something soothing and protective

Greet the water and thank it for its cleansing and healing. Ask it to soothe you and help you relax. Use the bath as a place to start your dream invocation, opening yourself to guidance and preparing for rest.

You can also do this as a loving and mindful shower by filling a bowl with just a handful of sea salt, warm water, and the optional flower water, and pouring it over your head as you shower.

Scent

Studies suggest that we sleep better and have better dreams when our environment smells good. Scent is so deeply linked to memory that this is unsurprising. If you like scent, consider using linen spray, or making your own with a few drops of essential oil in water in a glass spray bottle, and spritz your sheets and pillow. As you do so, invoke blessings for your sleep.

Some scents, like lavender, have studies backing their relaxing properties, but folks also have personal associations with scent, so if you are using a linen spray, burning incense or candles, diffusing essential oil, or applying perfume before bed, consider which scents you have positive and calming associations with. We made a list to get you started.

- Cedar—cleansing, grounding, protective
- Cinnamon—love, luck, prosperity
- Clary Sage—intuition, protection, relaxation
- Coconut—good luck, blessings, abundance
- Eucalyptus—purifying, connection to spirit
- Florida Water—protection, cleansing, blessing
- Frankincense—purifying, connection to spirit
- Geranium—wards off evil
- Heliotrope—devotion, harmony, innocence
- Jasmine—love, purity, strength
- Lavender—spirituality, peace, rest, psychism
- Lemongrass—clarity, protection, cleansing
- Lilac—love, luck, beauty
- Lily of the Valley—compassion, nurturing, spirituality
- Myrrh—purification, surrender, transition
- Nag Champa—breath of the spirit, meditation, peace

- Neroli—purity, new beginnings, happiness, love, hope, fertility
- Oud—divinity, purity, luxury, spiritual awakening
- Patchouli—love, fertility, healing
- Pine—protection, immortality, longevity, strength
- Plumeria (frangipani)—happiness, love, spirituality
- Rose—love, beauty, divinity
- Rosemary—memory/nostalgia, love, fidelity, sweetness
- Sandalwood—divine beauty, abundance, focus, blessings
- Spruce—good luck, protection, strength
- Sweet Basil—love, prosperity, protection
- Thyme—courage, strength, healing
- Vanilla—love, beauty, tranquility
- Vetiver—purification, grounding, balance
- Ylang-Ylang—luck, protection from evil spirits, love

Tea Time!

A cup of bedtime herbal tea is a nice evening ritual that is hydrating, relaxing, and comforting. There are practical reasons for bedtime tea as well—there are many herbs that promote good sleep, and some that have been traditionally used to stimulate dreams as well. Depending on your body, a cup of tea an hour or two before bed is ideal. We cover how to read the tea leaves in Chapter 6.

Please consult your doctor before adding any herbs or supplements to your diet. Some of these herbs, notably St. John's Wort, may be contraindicated with certain medications.

Evening herbs to consider:
- Ashwagandha—relaxation, mood, and adrenal support
- Blue Lotus—dreams and relaxation

- California Poppy—sleep, relaxation, and pain relief

- Chamomile—sleep, relaxation, and mood

- Hops—sleep and relaxation

- Lavender—sleep and relaxation

- Lemon Balm—sleep and relaxation

- Linden Flower—sleep and relaxation

- Magnolia Bark—relaxation

- Mugwort—dreams and protection

- Oat Straw—relaxation

- Passionflower—sleep and relaxation

- Skullcap—sleep and relaxation

- St. John's Wort—relaxation and mood

- Valerian—sleep and relaxation

Our Favorite Tea Recipes

For all of these, we like to keep it easy and use equal parts of the dried herbs, organic or pesticide-free if we can get it. We tend to use one table-spoon of each ingredient, mix in a bowl, and then transfer into a glass jar and label. Depending on the size of the jar, we might use two tablespoons or even three tablespoons of each ingredient—all equal parts. If you know you prefer more or less of something, or want to omit or substitute, go for it.

For one cup of tea, steep one tablespoon of the tea blend using a tea ball or unbleached tea bag in freshly boiled water for ten to fifteen minutes. You can cover the tea with a plate as it brews to keep it warm for longer.

Tea Ritual

As you are preparing the tea, aloud or in your head, greet and thank the plants that you'll be working with. We suggest experimenting with listening for a response from the plants. You can journal what you hear or record yourself.

As you're mixing and steeping the tea, state your intention aloud or internally. For instance, "I ask that these plants assist me in my sleep and dreams to _____."

Blow on the tea three times to infuse it with your intention.

When the tea is finished brewing, add whatever sweeteners you like, if you like them (honey, maple syrup, monk fruit, or stevia are recommended).

Drink while reflecting on your intention for what you would like to achieve with your dreams.

Jezmina's Bedtime Tea Recipes

These are some of Jezmina's favorite tea blends. You can further simplify or complicate these recipes according to your own taste. You can combine all of these in equal parts in a jar and scoop out a teaspoon in a teabag or tea ball and let the herbs steep for five to fifteen minutes.

Sleep Potion

- Ashwagandha
- Chamomile
- Mint
- Oat Straw
- Passionflower
- Poppy
- Skullcap
- Valerian

Floral Dreams

- Blue Lotus
- Chamomile

- Lavender
- Linden Flower
- Passionflower
- Rose Petals

Deep Dreams

- Blue Lotus
- Lavender
- Mugwort
- Oat Straw
- Passionflower
- Poppy
- Rose Petals
- Skullcap

Paulina's Tea Recipes

Paulina's recipes are simple and straightforward, and you can adapt these however you like as well.

Gypsy Milk

1 cup steamed milk or milk substitute
1 teaspoon dried lavender in a tea bag,
    steeped for 3 to 10 minutes and then removed
Honey to taste, if you like

Good Night Brew

Valerian root
Lavender
Chamomile
Honey to taste, if you like

Smoke Blends for Sleep and Dreams

There are lots of different brands of tobacco-free herbal cigarettes and loose smoke blends for spiritual/emotional support, and you can make them yourself.

Some people use cannabis or CBD as part of their sleep routine. If you do this, adding blue lotus, mugwort, and mullein to your smoke blend can be helpful.

If smoking or ingesting herbs isn't your preference, you can dab a drop of herbal oil on your forehead or your temples before sleep. This is a good option for people who are very sensitive to ingesting herbs. Blue lotus, lavender, and mugwort are nice options for sleep and psychism. In general, understand that essential oils are different from infused oils and are extremely concentrated, so essential oils need to be diluted with a carrier oil before being applied to the skin; some are not suitable for the skin at all. If you infuse your own oil, the blue lotus and mugwort are nice options. You can infuse herbs in oil by filling a clean, dry glass jar with the loose, dried herb all the way to the top, and pouring a safe carrier oil, like almond, grapeseed, olive, or sunflower depending on your preference, all the way to the brim of the jar. Label and date the jar, and shaking once a day, let the herbs steep in a cool, dark place, such as a cupboard, for three to six weeks. Then you can strain and reserve the oil using a fine mesh strainer or a cheesecloth to separate the herbs from the infused oil. Dispose of or compost the herbs.

However, please note that the essential oil of mugwort is highly toxic and made in a different process than the at-home infusion we describe. Essential oil of mugwort should never be used in your at-home smoke infusions.

Again, check with your healthcare provider for contraindications before smoking anything new.

Nightmares

Sometimes nightmares are productive and helpful because they bring fears that might have been repressed to the front of your consciousness. It's not healthy to repress your feelings. But sometimes nightmares are unhelpful symptoms of stress, trauma, PTSD, or other circumstances, and they feel like they're just repeating a pattern of suffering. If you struggle with nightmares that make it difficult to do dream divination, there are things you can try: lucid dreaming, therapy, meditation, ritual, and more. Both of us are believers in the healing power of a great therapist who's a good fit for you, so that's something to consider if you feel that you need some support.

Paulina's Adventures in Lucid Dreaming

I like to work with lucid dreaming to control bad dreams. I use a visualization trick that I learned when I was younger from one of the books at my family's shop, but there are many books on lucid dreaming, and many ways to practice it. I imagine that there is a ribbon hanging from the ceiling in front of my bed, and visualize what it would be like to pull on the ribbon as I go to sleep. I remain lying down, but I imagine how it would feel in my hand, what it looks like, exerting the muscles in my fingers, hand, and arm.

When I first began this technique, I kept doing this visualization as I was falling asleep until I could pull on a ribbon in my dreams. That's how I knew that I was dreaming when I was still asleep. Now that I have the power to control my dreams, if I'm having a nightmare, I can scream for help, or run away, or change the situation. This helps me feel more comfortable when it's time to dream.

Spiritual Practices for Dream Divination

Pull a Tarot Card for Sleep

Shuffle your deck and ask, "What can I do to give myself a more nurturing relationship to sleep?" and pull a card. Take three minutes and journal your thoughts in response to the card you pulled. For more information on Romani perspectives on tarot, take a look at Chapter 5.

Tarot as a Tool to Speak to Guides

Your guides could be spirit guides, angels, ancestors, deities, beloved dead … whatever you believe in. Shuffle your deck and ask, "What do my guides want me to know about my dreamwork?" Pull a card and journal for three minutes.

Easy Dream Sachet Spell

Fill a sachet with dried mugwort, rose, and lavender and place it under your pillow for good sleep and vivid dreams. You can also write down your intention for your dreamwork and slip that into the sachet, too. If you work with stones and crystals, you can put a small one in the sachet as well. Amethyst, quartz, and aquamarine are particularly effective for dreaming.

Setting Up a Dream Altar

A dream altar can be a formal or an informal thing. If you already have an altar that you work with, you can set your intentions for dreamwork there. You can also make a mini-altar close to where you sleep, like a bedside table or windowsill, with items that represent the intention of your dreamwork.

For instance, if you are working on healing your child-self, you might set up a small picture of yourself as a child, a rose quartz, and a small statue of a deity known for compassion, healing, and removing obstacles.

Setting Intentions for Dreaming

Go to your altar and communicate with whomever you are appealing to for guidance. That could even be your own wise self, or subconscious. You might like to light a candle, burn incense, or make an offering. Articulate your goals for dreaming.

Some intentions might be as follows:

- Abundance

- Advice

- Awakening

- Connection
- Creativity
- Direction
- Guidance
- Healing
- Insight
- Inspiration
- Integration
- Messages
- Processing
- Spiritual Growth
- Understanding
- Wishing

Record Your Dreams

Ideally, in many Romani families, you would discuss your dreams with a loved one or elder and work to make sense of them together, or just hold space for some processing. If you have someone who likes to talk about dreams and is a good processing partner for you, whether that's a friend, family member, or therapist, that's great. You could even start a monthly dream analysis club like Jezmina did. Talking it out can help you understand, but it's still good to write down or record what you dreamed and what you think it means. But not everyone loves to talk about dreams, and that's fine. Even if you're just writing out what you dreamed every morning, you're doing a lot.

Writing down or recording your dreams improves your recall, and you can keep a record of how they evolve over time. Certain themes, patterns, symbols, animals, plants, people, and metaphors might repeat, and you will learn to identify why, and what that means for your spiritual development and personal life. Keep a journal near where you sleep so you can write down dreams first thing, or write them on your phone, type them on your laptop, or record yourself. However you can take notes, it really helps, not just with your recall, but with your ability to identify signs and omens in your waking life too. If you're pressed for time in the morning, just summarize.

You will probably forget your dreams during the day, so try to get them down as soon as you can. If you miss a day, don't worry. Just do as much as you can.

What if I Just Don't Dream?

Sometimes people tell us this. Supposedly, we all dream, but some people have absolutely no recall. A small percentage of people go their entire lives without ever remembering a dream. Other people perhaps used to be able to but can't anymore, or seem to be able to recall them only sometimes. The ability to remember dreams can be affected by stress, sleep quality, drug/alcohol/medication use, genetics, and other factors. If you can't remember your dreams, now or ever, writing down your thoughts and feelings when you wake up can be just as valuable and might even help you conjure something from your nightly realms. You can also take up meditation and use that time as a kind of lucid dream state and write down your experiences.

What if I Know I Had a Dream, but I Don't Totally Remember It?

Try to jog your memory by asking yourself the following questions and journaling about anything you recall, no matter how vague:

- How did I feel emotionally in the dream?
- How do I feel now?
- What was the overall mood/vibe?
- Where was the dream set?
- Any details stand out?
- Was anyone else there?
- Was anything spoken?
- Any impressions I can recall?

What Does It All Mean? Journaling Questions to Ask Yourself

So you had a dream, and let's say you remember at least some of it. We bet it was weird. It can feel overwhelming to start the process of deciphering what it all means. Here are some helpful things to note in your journaling/recollection:

- What was the environment/setting?

- Who were the characters? What were they like? What was your relationship to them? How did you feel about them? Do you know them in real life?

- What were the major symbols in the dream? (important-feeling animals, plants, elements, objects, etc.)

- What were the feelings and emotions that you had in the dream?

- Were there any patterns, and what were they? (things/themes that kept coming up in this dream, and/or in other dreams)

If You Have a Dream Buddy

You can share perspectives with each other and ask questions similar to the journaling questions above to help each other look deeper. You don't have to have all the answers for each other about what it all means, but you can share thoughts and help each other look deeper.

Try not to project your opinion onto your dream buddy and just listen to their experience. Ask thoughtful questions to help them get to the meaning. Before offering an interpretation, ask for consent. They might want to just share and not hear your take. You might benefit from setting up some guidelines like this to make sharing easier and emotionally safer.

The Easiest Explanation Is Probably Correct

Sometimes we have stress dreams about things we're worried about, or better yet, wish-fulfillment dreams, or a number of other dreams that feel straightforward. It's still a good idea to write these down, and sometimes the details of them might give us insight into the minutiae of our feelings and associations. So, for instance, if you have a dream that you turn up naked at work, you're probably nervous about being made vulnerable at work. This is still helpful because there might be things you can do to make yourself feel more secure and grounded so this feeling doesn't persist. You can use divination tools, like oracle cards, tarot cards, or tea leaves, to help you dive deeper into what you need to feel settled if you're not certain. This would also be a great thing to problem-solve with supportive loved ones or a therapist.

The More Obscure Dreams

Then there are dreams that are more obscure. For instance, Paulina has had a recurring dream of nuns fully clothed sitting in a full bathtub with rubber duckies for years, and still isn't sure what it means. But she had another recurring dream about the devil that, over time, became clearer.

Paulina Fights the Devil

I used to dream that I had to battle the Devil in different guises to protect my family. As I got older, I understood it to represent my battle with the strictness of the Catholic religion I was raised with, and later, I found that it represented the different figurative battles I fought daily. The archetype of the Devil has different meanings in different religious traditions and spiritual paths, and its meaning changed for me over time too. I found that as I became less religious, I became more spiritual, and the Devil became more of a symbol rather than a literal idea of evil.

Jezmina's Crocodiles and Pumpkins

Some dreams feel like they need a Romani Sherlock Holmes to decipher them (or nearly any grandma). This one stumped me for a while, so I had to pull out all my analysis tricks to figure it out. We'll go through it step by step so you have a method to approach your own inscrutable dreams, but you're welcome to make any of our techniques your own.

I dreamed that I had adopted two crocodiles, and they were so unruly. One was thin and depressed, and the other was round and angry. I was stressed and wanted to give my new crocodiles away because they were getting aggressive with my friends and family. Then, at my house party where the guests and hostile crocs were mingling, someone tossed my crocodiles some pumpkins, and they munched them down, as happy and friendly as puppies. *Oh, my god, have I even been feeding my crocodiles?* I wondered. I felt deep shame and ran to get them more pumpkins. My crocodiles had a delicious meal, and I felt so close to them. When I woke up, I felt so emotional about the dream that I knew it was important, but I had to really think about what it all meant.

Start with Your Own Associations

The crocodiles felt like the most important aspect of my dreams, and I wanted to know what they symbolized. Since dreams are highly personal, your interpretations are the most accurate when they are rooted in your own references. It wouldn't make a lot of sense to start looking up what crocodiles represent in stories, mythologies, and cultures I wasn't raised with, since that would be very unlikely to appear in my subconscious. So I started with what I know about/associate with crocodiles.

My Auntie Susie used to read ancient Egyptian mythology to me when I was little, and I remembered that crocodiles represented fertility, creativity, and abundance, among other things. The thin crocodile reminded me of some of the drawings she showed me.

The crocodile in *Peter Pan* was both scary and intriguing to me when I was a kid because it was Captain Hook's nemesis, but was also a part of him, and vice versa. The round crocodile in my dream looked a lot like this one.

I used to live in Florida, and I was very afraid of an alligator eating my tiny feral Chihuahua mix, Lily, and at the same time, I loved seeing alligators in the wild.

My friend Michele loves alligators and crocodiles, and we sometimes took pole-dancing classes together when we attended grad school together for creative writing. I realized that I associate Michele with my more creative and healthy days, since I've been having health problems the last few years that have made it hard to write and dance, the things we did together.

A love of alligators is a major theme in her novel-in-progress, which I was reading a month or so before my dream.

Look at the Evidence and See What Resonates

I realized that the crocodiles are aspects of me for the following reasons:

I had been working on feeling more of my feelings around the time of this dream, which was about a year after my mother had died suddenly, and my father and I both tried to revive her with CPR. It took a year for me to even start to make sense of that, on top of falling very ill with long COVID-19 shortly before her death, which compounded some pre-existing health issues. My life had dramatically changed in a matter of a few months, and I was so ill after my mother's death that I was bedridden for a few months, and even afterwards, my mobility is so impacted by pain and exhaustion that, even now, I still walk with a cane.

Processing my grief, illness, and trauma was a good thing, but it was also unsettling. I was feeling angry more often, and sad, and I was much more expressive of my feelings and boundaries than ever before. I was also worried that my feelings were off-putting or upsetting to my loved ones. Sort of like unruly crocodiles and Captain Hook's nemesis.

Around the time of this dream, I had also been less creative than usual because chronic illness and grief take up a lot of energy. Sometimes I felt like that younger self who could physically do more was a better self, even though that younger self also repressed basically all of their feelings and still had their own struggles.

Nurturing the crocodiles actually made them happier, and I felt more loving toward them. Which is to say, telling myself that my younger self was better is cruel. Nourishing myself now, with all my feelings and sharp teeth, maybe brings me to a new type of creativity, healing, potency, and magic.

Wait, What Do the Pumpkins Represent?

The pumpkins are definitely nourishing, but how so? I needed to do some digging to find out what it meant to nourish myself according to this dream. I journaled about my associations with pumpkins, and realized that they conjure up fairy tales, magic, and autumn, the part of the year that deals in shadows and end of life. . . . I could keep going, but you can see how looking at your associations with even the most basic elements of a dream can be very helpful. I needed to bring magical practice into my life more, read the folktales I loved as a kid and maybe write some myself, tend to my inner child, and perhaps use these methods to help me cope with the loss of my mother and the dramatic change in my health. So many folk stories deal with trauma and grief, so returning to these stories as an adult was particularly cathartic.

The setting of the dream was a very cool swamp house on stilts surrounded by water, and I associate water with the subconscious, and with healing, like the Cups suit and the Moon card in tarot. Swamps are also a liminal space, the betwixt and between, where magical transformation happens. When someone important to you dies, it's natural to feel like you too are in a sort of underworld. Mythology tells us that heroes can return from that place, but they are always changed.

Moving Forward

The crocodiles are me, but I also felt like they might be a guide for me. I began paying attention to any mention of crocodiles or alligators turning up around me, and the context in which they appeared. I started regarding my uncomfortable emotions as hangry crocodiles who just need some pumpkins; in other words, when I was feeling upset, I practiced attending to my feelings rather than ignoring them. I also tried to give myself some grace around the fact that some of my sense of loss was connected to my lack of creativity and reduced mobility, so I gave myself more outlets that were appropriate for where I was. I wasn't ready to write a novel and hit a dance class, but I could listen to mythology podcasts and do gentle stretches in bed. I also made a conscious effort to reach out to family and friends who are nurturing, because it was a family friend in the dream who gave my crocodiles the first pumpkin and sparked my realization in the dream. Figuring out what a dream means is wonderful, but the most important part is deciding how to move forward with this new information.

Experiment

Dreams are nonlinear and use the language of the subconscious. They are a place of infinite exploration. We see parts of ourselves as characters or creatures, or scenarios, and examine them with less ego. If you want to draw more than one card or ask different questions, please do. These are just suggestions to get you started, and you are the expert on yourself anyway.

CHAPTER 4

The Basics of Palmistry

You sit across from your client in the light of flickering candles. You've both cleansed your hands with sanitizer and a few drops of Florida water, and the client extends their palm to you across the table draped in a jewel-toned tapestry. You hold their hand for a moment—such a compassionate, emotionally intimate act. We hold the hands of children, loved ones, the sick, the afraid, and as fortune-tellers, we hold the hands of clients too, sometimes dear people we've known for years, and other times complete strangers. In these moments, you take three deep breaths, and read with all of your senses.

Gifts of Palmistry

There are so many styles of palmistry and so many types of readers out there, but the two of us see palmistry as ideally suited to reading the past, present, and future, as well as the personality and nature of a person. Palmistry can be a broader kind of reading than tarot or tasseomancy, because those divinatory tools tend to shine for specific questions or intentions, or a focus on the present or future. Palmistry feels like the whole person, which makes sense because you are reading what's written on the body. And nothing is set in stone. You may have noticed that the lines on your palm will change over time, emphasizing how we make choices and can take different paths. Whereas the shape of our hands, which represents our natures and personality, tends to stay the same, but events can even influence this as well.

Palmistry balances who we are with what we can be, and learning the art of palm reading can help you unlock hidden knowledge about yourself and others. We are offering a sample of popular divination tools in this book, and there is so much more to say. We hope to share more in depth about palmistry in the future. Consider this chapter an introduction to the Romani perspective on the art.

Very Brief Palmistry History

Palm reading has its earliest roots in India, in Vedic astrology and Ayurvedic medicine, and was used to divine a person's personality and destiny, and even to diagnose or try to prevent health problems. The practice spread to China, Nepal, Tibet, and other parts of Asia through trade over the Silk Road. The mainstream spread of palmistry to the West can be traced along the same timeline and routes of the Roma's travel across the Middle East and into Europe and then the Americas.

Where to Start

Before you even start trying to interpret hand and finger shapes, lines, or symbols, you need to learn how to sit with the energy that a person holds in their hands. When you learn fortune-telling in a family tradition, you start by reading the people you're closest to, your parents, siblings, grandparents, aunties, uncles, and cousins—people you've probably known your whole life. This makes it a little easier to hold their hand and really feel their energy, the complexity of the person in front of you, their personality, aura, spirit, and way of being, with all their gifts, flaws, and quirks. Part of fortune-telling is being able to feel all that even for people you just meet, so it's helpful to practice on people you know, so you can see how the features of the hand map onto the features of the person.

Jezmina on Which Hand You Should Read

My grandmother said that the hand that feels the more dominant is your present life, and the less dominant is your most recent past life. If you are ambidextrous, go with the hand that you tend to write with. She said to read only the present life because "the past is garbage that you should have let go of already because you already died and moved on." I have to wonder if that philosophy has more to do with her traumatic past in this life than anything else. My grandmother had a "never look back" mentality that got her through a lot of extremely difficult experiences in her life, and she did not have many opportunities or support to reflect and start to heal, and sometimes people never get those opportunities. But in my opinion, if you have access to resources to help you process troubles, even if they happened a long time ago (in this life or another), it's best to use them.

In my own practice, I tend to focus on the present life because that's plenty to contend with, but I feel that past-life readings can be helpful if a person is repeatedly experiencing past-life memories or dreams that bother them. So in that situation, I will read the nondominant hand if the person needs help resolving those past-life experiences. Otherwise, though, I do stick to reading the dominant, or present-life, palm. I agree with my grandmother that, overall, the present is the place to be.

I don't believe that there is a right or wrong way to read palms, so read both or either if that feels best to you. My grandmother always emphasized that learning the rules of divination is one small part of being a good fortune-teller, and that being led by your own intuition is the most important.

Paulina on Which Hand You Should Read

My family also reads the dominant hand, but we will read the nondominant hand as well for longer, more in-depth readings. In my tradition, both hands represent the current life, and the nondominant hand just adds more information. We notice if the palms look similar or different, and the differences would show nuance in the person's character, or possibilities for their lives.

Practical Things You Can Tell from Someone's Hand

There are some obvious things that you can tell by holding someone's hands. For instance, if someone's hands are calloused and stained with motor oil, they're probably a mechanic of some kind. If someone's hands are extremely soft and well-manicured, they take a lot of care in their appearance and likely do not work with their hands. If their nails are bitten down to stubs, they are probably a very nervous person, or going through a hard time. There's nothing wrong with reading people from these commonsense indicators too.

Determining the Element of the Palm

Once you ascertain the overall feeling from a person, start to focus on the shape of the hand, and this will tell you about their personality. Palmistry uses the system of elements: earth, fire, air, and water. We all have all of the elements within us, but often a person's palm will show which element dominates them. Sometimes this aligns with your astrological sign, and sometimes it doesn't. It's a different system. But we all have all of the Zodiac within us too. We are great examples of this. Both of Jezmina's palms are dominant in fire, and Jezmina is a Leo, a fire sign, and even in the Chinese Zodiac, a Fire Tiger. So much fire. However, Paulina is a Cancer, a water sign, and a Wood Pig in the Chinese Zodiac, but neither of her hands reflect that. Her left hand is predominantly air, and her right hand is earth, and she is a righty. She feels that her personality is more earthy, but she aspires to be air.

And that's another fun thing! Humans are not perfectly symmetrical. It's possible to have two different elements for your two hands, or even to be a little between elements. Having hands that represent two different elements could reflect different sides of you, or depth to your personality, or your personality in this life versus the previous one, depending on how you read. Or all of the above.

Determining a person's element helps describe their nature, and many people benefit from learning more about themselves, even if they are very self-aware. A person's nature also affects the way that they approach different aspects of their lives, which is what the lines describe. So it's nice to start out with personality and nature to set the stage for the rest of the reading. Also, reflecting to a person what they are like generally is a gentle way to begin and helps build trust and comfort in you as a reader. Even if you're not giving someone a reading, being able to size up someone's personality by a quick glance at their hands can be useful.

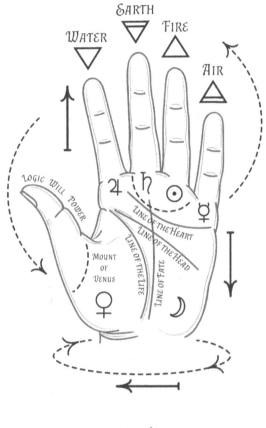

Earth

A square palm with short fingers and sturdiness to the hand indicates a dominance of the element of earth. Whether the hand is big or small, an earth hand has a healthy thickness to it. Folks with a lot of earth tend to be grounded, practical, and reliable, and they are usually good providers and caretakers. At their best, they are loving and compassionate, and tend to show it through action rather than words. Love is an action to them, and they are big on acts of service. They're going to bring you soup if you're sick, not just send you well-wishes. In the same vein, they tend to value people who are practical and show love through action as well. Words are cheap.

Earth hands also indicate someone who is a problem solver. They are good at fixing, making, creating, maintaining, taking things apart, and putting them back together. They're good at taking abstract concepts and making them concrete, and they can be very creative but are especially interested in how their creativity can be of use or of service. They might choose occupations like mechanic, builder, artisan, carpenter, sculptor, designer, or other jobs that make use of their hands, or their gifts of providing and fixing might show up in other ways, like mentoring or coaching.

Folks with earth are also known to be stubborn, and as two rebel types, we believe that stubbornness is sometimes what people label you if you're not doing what they want. Sometimes stubbornness is actually determination, resilience, and persistence, and these are all fine qualities. However, when stubbornness is getting in your own way, or it is destructive, self-sabotaging, or close-minded, that's when it becomes a problem. It's important for people with earth to stay connected to their compassionate nature and extend that loving energy to themselves. Let go of perfectionism and give yourself some grace.

Fire

A rectangular palm with short fingers and an average weight to the hand indicates someone dominated by the element of fire. This suggests a passionate person who is creative, warmhearted, and maybe a little impulsive and quick to anger. Fire folks are magnetic, charming, inspirational, and usually love to get things done and keep it moving, and they have high standards for themselves and others. They tend to have a lot of hot emotions, like excitement, joy, desire, anger, frustration, and the like, and they channel them into projects, work, communication, creativity, and more.

Fire hands are natural healers. They might become nurses or doctors, or otherwise work in medicine, or as healers like massage therapists, Reiki practitioners, teachers, counselors, or even chefs and artists. They tend to use their hands to heal in whatever capacity they choose, and if they don't do this at work, they do it in their personal lives. They're the kind of people who can give you a hug and say, "Honey, it's going to be okay," and you feel it through your whole body that yes, you're going to be okay. They are naturals at energy healing and often benefit from learning techniques for properly harnessing or channeling their gifts. They often have energy manifest in their hands as heat, even if they don't typically run hot.

Interestingly, fire has an inverse relationship to health, in that people with fire have a tendency to burn themselves out and overall ignore their own well-being. There's always something more important to do, more work to finish, someone to take care of. It's really important for folks with a lot of fire to pay close attention to their hot emotions, especially anger and frustration, in order to track when they've had enough, when they need a break, need to break up, need to quit, or need a nap and a snack. Listen to those needs. Remember, if you're fire, and you stay at raging bonfire levels, you'll be reduced to ashes. If you learn how to keep yourself at a nice, low flame, you will be unstoppable.

Air

Square palms and long fingers, and a palm that is slight and possibly even bony, indicates someone dominated by air. Often their hands are cool to the touch. This person is probably intellectual, quick-witted, curious, nervous, and very communicative. They might have an ethereal, philosophical way about them. Even if they are quiet by nature, they know how to turn on the charm when they must. They are often funny and observant, deal well with abstract concepts, and have many different interests. They like to keep their minds stimulated and to be around people who fascinate them. They are always learning, they like to understand others and the world around them, and they can be very logical and analytical.

Sometimes people with a lot of air are drawn to academia or intellectual professions, like writing, analyzing, researching, teaching, technology, and the like. However, no matter what they do, their minds are a great asset. They are good problem solvers and might have a talent for organizing, planning, and the like. They are also very good at adjusting to change, though they often fear it. They can also be a bit fickle themselves.

People with a lot of air have a tendency toward anxiety and overthinking, have a habit of intellectualizing their emotions, and can be dismissive of their own pain by rationalizing it away. This can be challenging because emotions need to be fully felt and accepted in order to be processed. Air will benefit from remembering that emotions have their own wisdom to offer, and it's okay for them to feel what they feel.

Water

A rectangular palm with long fingers, that looks overall narrow and elongated, indicates someone dominated by water. This person is likely intuitive, visionary, creative, compassionate, and imaginative. They're good at reading a vibe and reading a room, and tend to be very empathetic. They might be extra sensitive to other people's energies, so it's important for water to cleanse themselves regularly however they like, and practice envisioning a protective bubble, light, or shield around themselves so they don't take on the energy of anyone or any place.

Water is particularly good at holding space for people and helping them process their emotions. They might choose jobs that enable them to connect meaningfully with people and help them grow. Many water types are also artistic and might find themselves in creative work. Water is not always expressive through words and tends to keep a lot of their own emotions under the surface, so nonverbal outlets for self-expression, like art and dance, are important to help water process their feelings and get to that first step of communication.

They are very adaptable and great at landing on their feet no matter what kind of situation they're in. Water can make anything work. However, water can get caught up in people-pleasing. It's important that water remembers to value their own needs, dreams, and ambitions, and put their watery power behind their own goals, too.

Fingers

As with everything we share, there are going to be some Romani readers who teach palmistry differently. This is what the different fingers mean according to our families. We look at the shape of the fingers, if there are any lines or freckles on them, their flexibility, and if they curve one way or another to get more information about the person and their tendencies.

Finger Meanings

Each finger represents a different aspect of a person's life. The small fleshy pads at the base of each finger represent the ascribed meaning of each finger too, so you may see lines or lucky symbols there, and they would refer to the meaning of the finger.

The thumb is the seat of the will. Its flexibility or rigidity reflects one's personality. If you give a hard thumbs up, bending your thumb back as far as it will go, you will see how flexible it is. For example, if the thumb seems stuck straight up, this person is more rigid, and while they are probably very true to their values and have strong willpower, they might also be stubborn and not open to others' opinions or ways of doing things. If the thumb bends far back, however, this person is very flexible and open-minded, but may also be a bit of a pushover and struggle to advocate for themselves or uphold boundaries.

The index finger rules your direction, forward motion, and your ambition and ability to manifest. This finger has more to do with life path than career, though the two can be the same for some people. If this is the case, that a person's career and life path overlap quite a lot, they will often have an index finger that curves to the side toward the middle finger, usually at the middle joint of the finger.

The middle finger denotes how you are in business and your vocations, particularly those that earn you money or some other kind of abundance. If this finger is curved toward the index finger, it suggests that this person is very ambitious in their work, and perhaps motivated by titles, accolades, and prestige. If the middle finger curves toward the ring finger, it suggests that their work is very invested in good relationships with others, whether it's a client- or community-based career, family business or the like, or a career that allows for lots of time with family and loved ones.

The ring finger rules how you are in your relationships with the self and others. This finger governs all romantic, platonic, and all other relationships besides family. If this finger is curved toward the middle finger, it emphasizes a career built on good relationships. This person might enjoy working with their friends and find professional relationships very fulfilling. If it is curved toward the pinky finger, it suggests that this person likes to have deep relationships with creative people who help them feel more expressive and connected to themselves.

The pinky rules your creativity and spirituality. Creativity is different for everyone, and a lot of folks often undervalue their creativity or suppress it. It can look like arts, but it can also look like self-expression, hobbies, joyful pursuits, time with children, connection to nature, and anything folks do for fun. Spirituality is equally open-ended—for some people it's religion, for others it's their sense of values, purpose, cultural beliefs, philosophical outlook, connection to nature . . . spirituality is highly personal. Other elements of the palm will give context to how creativity and spirituality are expressed in the person. If the pinky is curved toward the ring finger, it suggests the person finds creative and spiritual fulfillment through their relationships. If it curves away, it emphasizes the person's independence in these areas.

Fingertip Shapes and Their Meanings

Fingertips are fascinating because sometimes our thumbs and fingers are uniform, and sometimes they have variation. Below are the most common types of fingertips and what they mean.

Spatulate: a finger that is square topped and flares out represents a natural leader, and someone who is determined, motivated, stable, logical.

Square: a finger that is square at the tips represents a practical, hard working, rational kind of person who is a good team member.

Conic: a finger that is elongated and comes to a tapered, almost pointy tip represents a person who is intuitive, emotional, ethereal, idealistic, dreamy, considerate.

Artistic: a finger that is rounded at the tip represents an empathetic person who is creative, inspired, imaginative, sensual, heart-led, and independent.

If you have all the same types of fingertips, it suggests that these qualities are true in all areas that the fingers themselves represent—will, direction, career, relationships, and spirituality and creativity. If there is a variety of fingertip shapes, then the above meanings correlate to what that finger represents.

Venus and Luna

Venus and Luna are two mounts on either side of the palm that represent us in community and rooted in the earthly plane, and us as individuals and our relationship to healing and the more mystical side of life. It can be interesting to compare the Mount of Venus and the Mount of Luna to each other to see what rules a person's life, and pay attention to where minor lines and symbols appear, which would relate to those areas.

Venus

There is a fleshy mound below the thumb that extends to the wrist. That whole muscle comprises the Mount of Venus in palmistry, and it represents your relationship to family, community, and ancestry. If it is very fleshy/developed, that suggests that community and family play a big role in the person's life. If it's flattened, then they are not such a big priority. If this area is sunken at any point, it can indicate grief about family issues or loss.

The horizontal lines that cross the Mount of Venus are a bit of a combination of ancestral influence and intuitive ability. Some readers interpret these lines differently, but one thought is that our ancestors and spirit guides aid us in our intuition, so that's why these lines appear here. If these lines are abundant and touch the life line, it represents a strong intuition. If the lines are sparse and patchy, it represents that the person might feel disconnected from their intuition sometimes.

If you extend your palm flat with fingers long and close together, the folds that appear at the base of your thumb represent intergenerational healing. Essentially, everyone has intergenerational trauma, but not everyone is focused on healing it all of the time. When these folds are especially visible and deep, the person is processing their feelings and wounds with respect to the traditions and beliefs they inherited, traumas or relationship patterns that were passed down, and more. These create opportunities for cycle-breaking. When there is an eyelike shape in the lines around these folds, encircling the folds, there is a protective mark, like the eye charms that ward off the evil eye, emphasizing how doing this intergenerational work protects you from harm and earns you the appreciation and added protection of ancestors who are in favor of this healing.

Luna

The muscle on the pinky side of the palm is the Mount of Luna, which spans about three-fourths of that side of the hand, from where the wrist meets the palm to the pad below the pinky finger. The Mount of Luna is your sense of self and independence, spirituality, philosophy, creativity, and connection to nature. If this side is very developed, this suggests a great importance in the person's life.

The Mount of Luna sometimes will have horizontal lines from the wrist to about halfway up the mount of Luna that represent spiritual practices that are beneficial to the person's life, which can be more or less overtly spiritual. These practices could include yoga, prayer, meditation, chanting, spell work, hands-on healing, or even quiet practices that are conducive to meditative or mindful states like nature walks, kayaking, knitting, beading, and more. A person with these lines benefits from spirituality through activities.

If there are horizontal lines on the side of the palm in the top half of the Mount of Luna, that represents spiritual or philosophical learning through study, reading, writing, and other scholarly methods. These lines usually appear between the end of the head and heart lines. A person with these lines might benefit from studying literature or texts that offer spiritual or philosophical perspectives on life. They thrive with intellectual stimulation on these topics.

The Basic Lines

There are so many potential lines and symbols in the palms, but here are some of the basic lines that you're likely to come across. The beginnings of lines also represent the beginning of the person's life, babyhood, childhood, and so on. The ends of lines represent old age, and eventually the end of life. Keep this in mind as a timeline when reading the basic lines. Remember that the palm is not set in stone. Lines change over time, as do people. You have free will and can make your own choices.

Life Line

The life line begins near the thumb and swoops around the Mount of Venus and represents your quality and trajectory of life in general, as well as your health. The beginning of the line also represents the beginning of a person's life, so babyhood and childhood are where the line starts near the thumb, and old age and the end of the life are where the line stops nearer the wrist. The length of your life line does not necessarily determine the length of your life, though a very short life line may indicate a risk-taker or even risk-seeking behavior, or health issues. People are often worried about their life lines being short, so it's good to reassure people that they're okay.

As you're reading this or any line, it's important to pay close attention to the quality of the line, which is covered in more detail later in this chapter. For instance, a smooth, deep, solid line suggests a relatively calm life that progresses more or less as expected. However, a line with forks or lots of off-shooting lines shows options and opportunities, and life changes that could take place. Sometimes it helps to ask a person's age to gauge how far along their life line they may be. You can also ask if a big life change that you see written on the palm has already happened to further pinpoint where they are on their life line. Branches or forks off the life line often point toward other parts of the palm, and that can give you more information.

A fork that veers further into the Mount of Venus on the thumb side of the palm suggests a chance that takes you closer to family or community. This can be something like working from home, or moving closer to family, or taking care of an elderly relative and moving them into your home. A fork that moves toward the Mount of Luna on the pinky side of the palm suggests striking out on your own path, prioritizing your independence, as well as your sense of purpose through career, creative fulfillment, connection to nature, or spirituality. Sometimes, if a life line forks in two, one path looks or feels more appealing than the other. A good path might be a deeper set line, or have lucky symbols on it like triangles or diamonds. A not-so-great path might be faint, have crosses over it, or many breaks. Often after a choice is made, the path you could have taken remains written on the palm for years, showing what could have been.

Life Line Beginning

Sometimes the beginning of the life line is combined with the beginning of the head line, like two rivers that share a source. When these two lines are connected at the beginning, it suggests that the person is especially imaginative, visionary, intellectual, and curious even from an early age. It's likely that as a child they were always reading, writing, drawing, or dreaming, or taking appliances apart and putting them back together, fixing things, building things, planning, and always thinking. If the person's childhood is particularly difficult, which would be indicated by a number of small crosses over the line, this could also represent a degree of dissociation or escapism as a coping mechanism. Most people have some crosses over the beginning of their life line because childhood is challenging for most people. Be sensitive about this subject if you're discussing it with the person whose palm you're reading. They might not want to dive into childhood hardship, so it's important not to be prying or needlessly blunt.

Two or More Life Lines

Sometimes people have two life lines or, very occasionally, more. It's most common to have a short life line and a longer one, and this represents having overcome tremendous hardship, or even a near-death experience. This could be anything from surviving abuse or becoming sober after an addiction, to surviving a serious accident, attack, or suicide attempt. The metaphor is that the person has risen up after death. This is similar to the Judgment card in tarot in that way. If there are a few shorter lifelines and one longer one, this experience has happened more than once. Since this is such a personal and sensitive topic, we recommend focusing on the person's resilience, not their trauma. You can acknowledge that they have overcome a lot without making them feel exposed. This is the mark of a survivor. Celebrate their ability to beat the odds.

Double Life Line

This is different from having two or more life lines. This is when your life line has another right up close next to it, like a shadow. The double line can be through the whole life line, but sometimes the two integrate at some point. Some readers see this as a sign of good health and longevity. Others read it as a person who feels like they have two sides that they move through the world with. Maybe they need to present one side of themselves to family but can be more themselves with close friends (or vice versa). Maybe they have one persona at work, and another for their personal life. There's nothing wrong with keeping parts of yourself private, but it can be exhausting, especially if you're keeping secrets for fear of discrimination. It's always nice when the person has the opportunity to be more fully themselves most of the time, and not only parts of themselves sometimes.

Fate Line

The fate line generally runs through the center of the palm, starting somewhere below the middle finger and moving toward the wrist. This line represents career and vocation, and can include your job, parenting, hobbies, or anything that you pour a lot of time and energy into that adds to your abundance in some way.

If the fate line veers toward the Mount of Venus and the life line, this suggests the person will be in a career that's oriented toward community service or family. If the fate line veers toward the Mount of Luna, this suggests the person will have a career that is in some way self-directed and emphasizes their independence. Their work might also be influenced by creativity, spirituality, and/or nature as these are the star attributes of the Mount of Luna.

Sometimes the line doesn't seem to start until further down the palm, and if you look closely where you would normally expect to see the beginning of the fate line, there's usually a collection of tiny, soft lines instead. This means that the beginning of the fate line is dispersed, like steam over a lake. It means that the person's work experience at the start of their life might be varied, or that their first job, or first few jobs, required them to do a little bit of everything. This can be helpful because the person might have a broad skill set. Other times, a person's fate line is dispersed the whole way down, like instead of a solid line they have a collection of faint rivulets. The absence of a line indicates no set path. This emphasizes someone who thrives when they have lots of options, variety, the ability to flow, maybe even work several different jobs at once, or work one job that offers them flexibility.

Head Line

The head line may or may not be joined to the life line and extends horizontally across the palm toward the Mount of Luna. It begins on the thumb side of the palm and ends on the pinky side. It represents your mental life, ranging from studies, intellectual pursuits, and rationality to mental health. For some people, the head line is extremely long, extending from one side of the palm all the way to the other, and that indicates someone for whom learning and study are very important. They might pursue multiple degrees or choose a field where there is constant learning, or they might be self-taught well into their old age.

If the head line dips down far toward the wrist, it suggests that the person struggles with self-doubt, which can even stop them from pursuing the intellectual path they truly want. It's helpful to remind folks with this kind of head line that the only thing standing in the way is their confidence, and they are perfectly capable of anything they put their mind to.

If the head line is straight across, it suggests that the person has a pretty accurate measure of what they're capable of, and may even excel in tests of logic and rationality.

If the head line turns up toward the pinky, which is unusual, this suggests the person is extremely optimistic and has perpetual rose-colored glasses on, even when it doesn't seem reasonable to see life that way.

If there are forks or branches off of the head line, it suggests adding new areas of study. For some people, this might correspond with the fate line. A new career shown in the fate line might be mirrored in the head line if it requires a new degree or certification in a different field. Sometimes a person will have lots of tiny branches off of their head line, and that is likely someone with many interests, and that can be a really lovely way to live life. Encourage curiosity and learning.

If the head line seems to end and then faint lines begin to extend, it means that the person is thinking about pursuing school or study again, or furthering their study in their chosen field in some way, and it's good to give them encouragement to do this. The extending line appearing suggests that it's a good and possible path.

Heart Line

The heart line generally begins right between the base of the middle and the index finger, or somewhere below there, and extends horizontally across the palm and toward the Mount of Luna. It represents all of your emotionally close relationships other than family, whether they are platonic, collegiate, or romantic. This line shows how you are in social and/or romantic relationships, how you are affected by them, and what your lessons and tendencies are. Sometimes people come to you for a reading and are a bit fatalistic or obsessive about their true love or soul mate and the longevity of their relationship. It's important to remind them that this line, like all the others, will change over time, and that love involves other people's free will, so predicting their love life events is not as important (or accurate) as examining how they are in relationships and what they can work on for happier love connections.

If the heart line starts right between the middle and index finger, this usually represents someone who is independent, perhaps ambitious in love, with pretty good boundaries and high expectations of themselves and others. Sometimes you'll see sketchy lines that look like the heart line once started lower on the palm and has since extended upward, so this suggests that the person has become this way over time through experience.

If the heart line starts further down on the palm, this usually represents someone who needs a lot of love and attention, is openhearted but maybe a little self-involved, sees the best in people, gives second (third, and fourth . . .) chances, and might struggle with boundaries. It's great to be open and see people's potential, but it's really important to have boundaries too. Usually this person would benefit from the reminder that having needs and boundaries with loved ones means being honest with them, and it gives your loved ones opportunities to show love and care by acknowledging those needs and respecting those boundaries.

Sometimes the heart line will start with a big fork or split, and that can represent the painful effects of a breakup or divorce. If one branch of the fork reaches back toward the beginning of the life line, it suggests that the person is working through childhood trauma around love, trust, and relationships as well. A wonderful thing that can happen is that lucky symbols, like diamonds (representing abundance), often appear here over time, closing the split, which suggests that the person has learned to value and require the concrete, tangible efforts people make to be good partners or friends.

In addition to the love line representing many types of love and not just romantic love, remember that some people identify as ace (or asexual) or aro (aromantic) and might not be interested in sexual or romantic relationships at all, or might be sexual and not romantic, or romantic and not sexual. Or they could be gray ace and fall somewhere on the spectrum of asexuality and allosexuality (experiencing sexual attraction). So you don't have to explain everything on the heart line in terms of romantic love. Also, many folks are LGBTQIA+. Don't assume anything about gender or sexuality, especially with regards to this line. People deserve to feel comfortable and accepted during readings without having to do the work of coming out to a reader. Some people are monogamous and some are poly. Sometimes people are straight up cheating and need a nonjudgmental space to talk about it. It's not our place to assume or make judgments.

Don't Have a Separate Head and Heart Line? You Have the Line of Achievement

This is a line that a person would have in place of the head and heart line. Usually this is one horizontal line that extends from one end of the palm to the other, and it is an usual characteristic that is said to mark the individual for greatness. As you might imagine, the metaphor is that the heart and head line are combined, making the person particularly ambitious and able to prioritize their goals over their relationships, if needed. However, some people's goals include fostering loving relationships, so we all have the ability to make choices.

Child/Marriage Line(s)

These are short horizontal lines on the side of the palm below the pinky. Traditionally, the number of lines represents how many children you'll have, or in some traditions, how many marriages you'll have. If you're the kind of reader who sees these as child lines, keep in mind that they are not always biological children or even literal children. We tend to say that they represent you being a positive influence on young people, whether you're a parent, family member, teacher, mentor, or otherwise around children in some other way.

Qualities of the Lines

Everyone's hands are unique, so there is a lot to consider. One factor is the quality of the lines themselves. In the same way that you would analyze brushstrokes in a painting, consider whether the lines are deep or faint, constant or broken, crossed or smooth. Reading a person's energy is so important in palm reading so it's important to feel out what this could mean. For instance, a thin line for one person can mean something different for someone else. Here are some common types of lines and what they mean.

Deep
When a line looks deep on a person's palm, it indicates how important that facet of their life is to them. If all of the lines are deep, it suggests someone who lives life with a lot of passion and dedication.

Smooth
Lines that are smooth with few (or no) breaks, branches, chains, crosses, or other disruptions reflect a person's focus and relative ease on their path.

Thin and Light
Very faint or thin lines, particularly for the major lines like life, heart, head, and fate, suggest a tenuous relationship to that part of a person's life. This could be that the person might not prioritize what's represented by those fainter lines, or that they take a more airy, ethereal, or intellectual approach to those areas of their life.

Crisscrosses
Lines with many crisscrosses over them can suggest times of difficulty. These often appear at the beginning of the life line because it can be hard to be a kid sometimes even in the best circumstances—there's so much change and learning happening, and then add childhood trauma and it

gets very complex. These are also areas where lucky symbols can appear, however, because sometimes we make strengths out of our struggles.

Broken

Lines that have gaps, or that stop and then pick up later, can represent times of illness or other periods of transition that are challenging. For instance, a gap in the career line could be losing a job, or having to quit for some reason, and then taking a moment to know what to do next.

Branches

Branches are long or short lines off of a main line that can represent changes or influences. For instance, a collection of short branches off of the heart line can represent significant relationships (platonic or romantic). Short branches off the fate line might be projects, contracts, side hustles, or gigs. A long branch off the head line might be a degree or a certificate in a new subject, but a short one could be a new area of interest for more casual study.

Chains

Lines with chains or islands denote a period of solitude, transformation, stepping away from and coming back to the self, a path, or others. This can be positive, negative, or neutral. When these appear on the heart line, it often represents periods of time when the person needs more solitude, even if they're in a loving and committed relationship. A chain on the life line could be an intense period of self-discovery, and on the fate line it could be a break like maternity leave or a sabbatical.

Minor lines

These are some of the more commonly seen lines that only some people have.

Creativity

The creativity line, extending diagonally from the pinky across the Mount of Luna toward the center of the palm, suggests an artistic and intuitive person. There can be more than one. Sometimes people would rather fight you than accept that they are creative, so it's helpful to remind people that creativity means a lot of things: arts, expression, creative problem solving, joyful hobbies, fixing things, entertaining, keeping a home, or anything you do for fun.

Fame

The fame line extends from the ring finger toward the heart line and it suggests a person who may have some amount of fame, visibility, reputation, or popularity. It also suggests an intensity in relationships if it touches the heart line, and it may mark when that intensity begins in a relationship with the self or others. Fame is relative and doesn't mean celebrity. A farmer might have an amazing fame line if they donate food to the shelters and schools in their community. They have a great reputation for doing good deeds.

The Girdle of Venus

The Girdle of Venus is a semicircular line that swoops (broken or unbroken) from the base of the index finger to the base of the ring finger and suggests an emotional, sensitive, and sensual person sharing the gifts of spiritual love and beauty. The idea is that they are blessed as though by deities of love and beauty, and that is their spiritual path. They may have a romantic outlook, a strong sense of aesthetics, and love sharing beautiful experiences with their favorite people. A broken Girdle of Venus suggests that there is some healing or work to do before the person can fully use their gifts.

Balance

A vertical or diagonal line that connects the head and heart line suggests the two are in balance.

Skills

The skill lines running horizontally across the wrist are artisan/craftsperson lines and suggests something that the person is/can be skilled at making/creating. The more lines, the more skills, and the further up the arm they go, the more you learn as you age.

Lucky Symbols

These are shapes or symbols that can appear anywhere on the palms: on or over the lines, on the pads below the bases on the fingers, on the mounts of Venus and Luna . . . really anywhere. And the area that they appear in indicates what kind of luck or blessing it is.

Triangles

If there is a triangle that sits on a line, it represents a time of empowerment in that area of the person's life. Like climbing a mountain peak, it takes work, but you accomplish something important.

Diamonds or squares

Whether it's a diamond or square is a matter of perspective, but they represent prosperity, stability, and abundance.

Evil Eye

An eye shape represents protection from harm. This can appear anywhere on the palm, but it's always interesting to see what aspect of a person's life is protective.

Cross

A single cross connecting the heart and head lines suggests magical ability, like psychism. A single cross elsewhere on the palm, not on a line, can be a blessing, though it might not always suggest ease. It's like a burden that becomes a blessing.

Star

A shape or mark that looks five pointed, like a star, or even like an asterisk, is an indication of intense power, and change that is messy but extremely fortunate.

The Palm as a Whole

There is so much more to dive into with palm reading: many more lines, symbols, variations. We wanted to give you an overview and introduction to the subject to give you a sense of how Roma approach palm reading in general. You will find that the more you gaze at a palm and open yourself to the person's energy, the more you sense. It's always fascinating to see symbols in the palm that you don't see in any text, like lines that converge to look like bears, fish, or leaves, or any other image. As you are reading, you suddenly piece together what that means for the person before you.

For instance, Jezmina once saw a symbol of a bear in a client's palm; it was sitting in front of the heart line, looking out at the start of the life line. For the client, the bear was guarding them from repeating early painful experiences in their love life again, and felt like the presence of a protective ancestor with their best interests in mind. Your intuition will help you understand what it all means with practice. Consider this chapter a jumping off point.

CHAPTER 5

The Basics of Tarot Reading

You ask your client if they have any question in mind, or if they just want to see what message the cards have for them. They tell you they're open to anything, so you take deep breaths as you shuffle nine times, listening to the rhythmic thwacking of the deck arranging and rearranging itself. You're conjuring feelings of empathy and connection for the person sitting in front of you, calling on your ancestors, angels, guides, and God to help you see what must be seen, and say what must be said in a way the querent can hear it.

A Very Brief History of Tarot

The first tarot decks were created in Italy around 1430, and they were intended to be a card game. Roma invented tarot reading and cartomancy in general as a job upon their arrival in Europe and popularized it across Europe and the UK, particularly throughout the 1700s–1880s. As you might remember from our history chapter, Roma were met with intense discrimination at this time in Europe, which continues today. Now that tarot, our survival trade, has become so trendy, it's especially important to support and spotlight Romani readers and teachers who have mostly been erased, whitewashed, or misrepresented in mainstream occultism, and are far more likely to be accused of scams than their white counterparts, directly because of centuries of ingrained racism.

What a lot of people consider to be the standard modern tarot deck is based on the Venetian or the Piedmontese tarot. It consists of seventy-eight cards divided into two groups: the Major Arcana, which has twenty-two cards, also known as trumps, and the Minor Arcana, which has fifty-six cards. One of the most popular decks is the *Rider-Waite-Smith*, first published in 1909. Its popularity is partly because it is in the public domain, meaning it's no longer protected by copyright, so anyone can do their own version of it. As such, there are many artistic interpretations of this deck out there, so it's a good one to learn. The person responsible for the iconic imagery of this deck is Pamela Colman Smith (February 16, 1878–September 18, 1951), also nicknamed Pixie, who was a Black British artist, illustrator, writer, publisher, and occultist. She is best known for illustrating the Rider-Waite tarot deck for Arthur Edward Waite, but she was not credited at the time. Colman also illustrated over twenty books, wrote two collections of Jamaican folklore, edited two magazines, and ran the Green Sheaf Press, a small press focused on women writers.

Paulina's Tarot Journey

My mother would usually make me watch her give tarot readings almost every day. When my aunts came into town, she would make me sit in on their readings, and when we visited my grandmothers, she would make me listen to their readings too. This must have been a little weird for the person receiving the reading, being shadowed by a nine-year-old, but that's just what we did. It was a family business. My mother said there is no such thing as learning too much information. Both my parents would make me ask all the women in the family at least one question about how they read any time we visited.

Once I got a little older, around twelve, my mom not only explained the meaning of each card, but told me to read every book in our shop on tarot, and so I did. I realized the meanings my family had for tarot were not always the same as what I read in books. I realized the meaning of tarot cards and suits also varied in each book I read. I realized meanings even varied between readers. All I knew was I had so much information, and, when asked about the meanings of the cards and suits, it was from one of those sources, all of those sources, and my own feelings at the same time.

What I learned from sitting in readings was that you can look at a card and just tell the meaning based on the colors, and that's the right way. You can look at another card and speak badly about it because you didn't like the way it felt when you pulled it out of the deck. All the ways are correct because it's a spiritual practice, and not a perfectly formulated method. In our house, we read so many cards, the decks would often be damaged, burned, and mixed with at least four other decks. I remember one time pulling out four Tower cards in one reading, and all I could think was, *this person is in for a wild ride.* The deck was so mutilated, but that was the beauty of it, because it was still the right way.

Jezmina's Tarot Journey

My grandmother actually preferred to read regular playing cards rather than tarot, so those were the cards I started reading too. I actually thought that all Roma preferred playing cards for a long time until I learned otherwise. When my grandmother first moved to the United States, she was nineteen and didn't speak any English, and she moved in with her new husband and his elderly mother. The first gift her mother-in-law gave her to welcome her to this country was a pack of fortune-telling cards, which were like playing cards but they had cryptic little fortunes scrawled on them such as, "a woman with dark hair is jealous of you," or "good news comes your way," or "you will never marry the one who loves you ardently."

My grandmother never spoke about it directly with her new mother-in-law, but she felt that this was the woman's way of showing that she accepted my grandmother for who she was, a Gypsy foreigner, and even liked her for it. As such, this became my grandmother's most precious deck, and the only one that she would read with from then on. The cards helped her learn English, connect with her new family, and not feel so homesick. By the time I learned to read with this pack of cards, they were so tattered and worn that we didn't even risk shuffling them anymore. We just gently swished them around in a pile on the table, and gathered them back up again ever so carefully.

I noticed that my grandmother didn't always go by the meanings inscribed on the cards when she was reading them, those ready-made fortunes written on the tops and bottoms of each card. "You have to feel what the card means," she shrugged. "It's different depending on who's asking, what they asked, and which cards lie around each other." She got annoyed when I wanted to write down all the meanings so I could memorize them. "I don't know what good that will do you," she scoffed. Learning the cards was clearly more involved than just knowing what they mean. Having to write them down was like cheating to her—she expected me to know them from my soul, not my mind. So I practiced with her and watched her read for family and friends. I would hover over their readings and ask lots of questions, and then I would try myself, and the more I saw combination after combination of cards unfold, the more the many possibilities and messages seeped into my bones so it felt like second nature.

When I was twelve, I asked if I could start learning tarot because it seemed more common among gadje than playing cards, and I thought I would do better business if I could use a tarot deck. "Sure," she said. "It's all the same." She firmly believed that if I meditated, cleansed, protected, and prayed how she taught me, I would just absorb the meanings of the cards. And honestly, she was right. I showed her the tarot deck I was using and got her opinion on the meanings, and practiced reading for her and family under her critique. I read about the tarot meanings from different authors, and they were sometimes similar to the corresponding playing cards or my grandmother's opinion, and sometimes they were different. The playing cards are sassier, and more direct. If you think tarot cards call you out, they're nothing compared to playing cards. I find tarot offers more symbolism to chew on, but in Romani fashion, I still like to get right to the point, even in my tarot readings.

My grandmother was a big believer in never admitting if you forgot a card or got confused if you were reading for someone you needed to impress, like a client or someone who could become one. She would say there are no accidents, and your confidence is more important.

Romani meanings and descriptions within tarot are more to the point and straightforward. There are also more realistic interpretations rather than all "love and light" seen today by many non-Romani practitioners.

—April Wall, author of *Reading Tarot, Reading Tea Leaves,* and *Deciphering Angel Numbers*

Selecting a Deck

No one needs to buy a deck for you, unless you like that superstition. It's important that you are drawn to the artwork because that is what you will be inspired by as you're reading. The symbols are meaningful. You can see if any deck "calls" to you—some people feel warmth from the deck, or feel literally pulled toward it, or just good vibes. You can have more than one deck. It's okay to pick something just because it's pretty. A lot of people like to start with the classic Rider-Waite-Smith since, once you learn that deck, it's very easy to learn any others based on it. It's a nice idea to consider the creators you want to support, and avoid decks that are culturally appropriative. We are passionate about supporting Romani- and BIPOC-created tarot and oracle decks. Some of our favorites are decks illustrated by Romani and Indigenous artist and witch Katelan Foisy, who collaborated on decks with Black and Indigenous creator and author Tayannah Lee McQuillar, such as *The Hoodoo Tarot* and *The Sibyls Oraculum*. Katelan Foisy also frequently collaborates with Billy Corgan of The Smashing Pumpkins. We also love *The Living Altar* by Ylvadroma Marzanna Radziszewski and Kiki Robinson, a queer-, trans-, Romani-made oracle deck with spells that accompany each image.

When you're just starting, it can be difficult to learn from super simplified tarot decks because it helps to have some symbols to hang onto when you're a beginner. A well-made tarot deck will be rich in symbolism and tell you what the cards mean without having to refer to a text, though it's nice to read about different interpretations. Symbols are born of culture, lore, stories, mythologies, and more. Take some time with each card, noting not just the major symbols, like wands, cups, pentacles, and swords, but the minor symbols that are woven into the artwork. Some of them will be well-established, and others you might ascribe a new meaning to, and that meaning might change.

Tarot versus Oracle Cards

A tarot deck is a deck composed of a major and a minor arcana, making up seventy-eight cards, and while there are interpretations of the card meanings and imagery, the cards are more or less set. Oracle decks have a lot more flexibility according to the artists and creators who make them. They can have any art, any words, phrases, meanings, or themes. Reading with tarot, playing cards, Lenormand, oracle, and the like all fall under the umbrella of cartomancy, but for the purposes of this chapter, we're focusing on an introduction to tarot. Oracle cards can be a wonderful accompaniment to a tarot reading as an intention card for the beginning of a reading or a closing message at the end, or however else you want to incorporate them.

Storing Your Deck

Jezmina's grandmother insists that cards prefer to be wrapped in soft fabric, like silk or satin, and that they must never touch a bare table or floor without a cloth or doily between. She believes that if you drop the cards, or have to place them on a less than perfect surface, you should apologize. In our opinion, it's fine to keep them in the box though, especially if you're traveling between gigs and need to keep them safe and organized. And we've both used cards on a bare table before, and no disastor struck. As long as you treat your cards with respect, you're good to go, even if they get a little battered along the way. As you can tell from both of our reflections on learning this craft, cards can take a beating, and that's to be expected. Just be nice to them, even if you accidentally catch them on fire.

How to Shuffle and Choose a Card

The good news is that there's no wrong way to do this. Whether you shuffle like you're dealing a hand of poker, or you swish them around gently over a lace tablecloth, the important thing is that you are shuffling the way you prefer and using the action of shuffling as an opportunity to clear your mind and connect with the cards and any other divinity or wisdom you wish to call in. As you're shuffling, you can practice the cloud meditation, or just breathe deeply as you focus your energy on the task at hand.

Both of us coincidentally like to shuffle cards in threes. So we shuffle three times, and if that doesn't feel enough, then we shuffle six times, and if six doesn't do the trick, then it has to be nine times. Notice whatever lights up your brain or hands when you're shuffling and do what you like. Paulina likes to draw the cards from the top of the deck when she finishes shuffling, but Jezmina likes to cut the deck in two piles and then choose which to draw from based on how they feel, also starting from the top. You can do whatever you feel you like. Experiment to see what you like the best.

Tarot Symbolism

There are so many different decks with different interpretations, and schools of thought on what the major symbols mean, that it can feel overwhelming. Where do you start?

- Read different dictionaries and encyclopedias of symbols, and read mythology and folklore from all over the world.

- Consider what is your relationship to the symbols in the tarot—are you able to perceive and also set aside your own associations with the symbol? Be neutral. Take the concepts of good and evil, for instance. Morality is relative, dependent upon context, circumstances, options, perspective, and more. Good and evil are not set in stone, but they do test your character.

- Pay attention to polarizing cards that feel extreme, either extremely good like the Sun, or extremely bad like the Devil, but remain neutral and curious with each card and experience. No card is all good or bad. Life is complex, and the cards represent that. They all come with their poison and their cure.

Diving into The Moon

Let's take The Moon card as an example. It's so rich with mystical symbolism, so it's a great card to do a deep dive with. Begin by gazing at this illustration of The Moon and try to identify as many symbols as you can, and make some notes about what you think they mean. Draw your own conclusions before you look up the meaning in a book.

Common Symbols in The Moon Card

- The moon—reflection, lunacy, dreams, psychism, goddess energy, power, intuition, emotions, cycles, changeability

- The ocean—the subconscious mind, repressed emotions like fear, emotional depth, shadow work, life force, the unseen, the hidden

- The crab—the astrological sign of Cancer, crossing liminal spaces, emerging from the subconscious into the conscious, between worlds (land and sea)

- The dog—a guide, humanity, kindness, perceptiveness, compassion, civilized/domesticated

- The wolf—madness, wildness, untamed, survival instinct, animal impulse

- The two towers—polarity, "good and evil," sanity and madness, perception and paranoia, truth and delusion

Textbook Meaning versus Intuitive Meaning

Certain aspects of the cards will be more important depending on the reading or context. In one reading, The Moon might emphasize that you need to slow down and process some deep feelings. In another, it may warn that the person is letting delusion get the best of them. This is where your intuition comes in, as well as any clarifying cards.

How to Work with a Card Intuitively

- Shuffle your deck of cards and take at least three deep breaths, perhaps using the cloud meditation or another technique for clearing your mind.

- If it's in your practice, invoke your guides, ancestors, deities (whoever) to aid you as you intuit a message from the card.

- When you're ready, ask the deck to show you a card that you need to learn from, and select a card in your preferred method.

- Gaze at the card you selected as you keep your deep breaths steady. Take in all symbols you can see and send your awareness into all aspects of the card, almost as though you could transport yourself inside the image.

- Which parts of the card speak to you the loudest? Which symbols stand out the most? What do you notice when you dive in deeper? Take some notes in your journal to help yourself get into the flow of your exploration.

- Hover your hand over the card and go inward, by either closing your eyes or softening your gaze. See what you can sense physically or emotionally from the card. Take notes on this experience.

- Continue to open all of your senses and keep your breath steady. Notice what changes in your sensory landscape and trust the information that you receive. Take notes.

- Be curious, and start to engage your intellectual process. Explore all the information that is available to your senses, and start to piece it together for a more concrete meaning. Take notes.

- When you've intuited as much as you can, you can look up the meanings from a few different sources and see what resonates with you.

Learn the Meanings but Prioritize Intuition

It's important to know what the cards mean, but anyone can memorize seventy-eight cards. It's essential to practice feeling and intuiting what the cards mean at the time you are working with them, as the meaning changes depending on the question, person, time, and so on. Establish a daily spiritual practice of cleansing, communing with spirit or source, quieting your mind, and opening your clairsenses.

If you're reading in an informal setting, like by yourself or practicing with friends, it's absolutely okay to look up meanings to help you memorize what the cards mean in context. We really enjoy tarot resources by Romani writers April Wall and Lisa Boswell, whom we've mentioned earlier. We also love to read widely and have enjoyed books by gadje, like *Seventy-Eight Degrees of Wisdom* by Rachel Pollack, *78 Acts of Liberation* by Lane Smith, and many others. It's a good idea to look at different interpretations of the cards from different sources and decide what feels most resonant with you over time. April Wall remarks that everyone has ability, but "as with any ability or talent, some are born with a higher aptitude for it, but I believe with practice and training anyone can learn how to work with divination. Not everyone can be the Beyoncé of Tarot, but the world still needs Michelles and Kellys." Even if you are looking up tarot meanings always and forever, it can still be a powerful and valuable practice for you.

We could write a whole book on tarot, or any of the divination topics we introduce, and we hope to share more in the future. Consider the rest of this chapter our guide for navigating the tarot and remembering the meanings in a pinch.

The Major Arcana

These twenty-two cards are heavyweights—they weigh more in a reading, meaning they anchor or color a spread, because they represent major themes and symbols in our life. The first card is The Fool, represented by the number 0 because it represents the infinite, the space beyond space, the beginning before the beginning. You can think of each of the subsequent cards of the Major Arcana as the Fool's Journey. The Fool is openhearted, ready to learn, starting from nothing but held by the universe. This is what it is to be on any journey of growth and healing. Each card that follows represents an experience or lesson for The Fool and further transforms them. The last card of the Major Arcana is The World, number 21, another card of infinite possibility, but one supported by experience. It is the end of one journey and the beginning of another. There is a beautiful film by Tony Gatlif titled *Latcho Drom* (*Safe Journey*) that recreates the long migration of Roma over the centuries from Northwestern India to Spain. The film documents this journey primarily through music and dance, and it has very little dialog, and in this way, the film's artistic depiction of the Romani diaspora offers the viewer the opportunity for a slightly different interpretation each time. We think of the journey through tarot in a similar way. We are all on a long road, hoping for safe travels, navigating the beauty and tragedy of life, and still making it our own.

Keywords for the Major Arcana

We have some keywords for the Major Arcana that can be helpful for you to remember, keeping in mind that interpretations vary person to person, and reading to reading.

0—The Fool—new beginnings, dive in with an open heart, inexperience, luck in new endeavors

1—The Magician—manifesting, creation, resourcefulness, using all the tools available to you

2—The High Priestess—spiritual leadership, intuition, solitude, wisdom, trust in the universe and yourself

3—The Empress—leadership, nurturing, fertility, power

4—The Emperor—dominance, power, leadership, control

5—The Hierophant/Pope—learning, teaching, tradition, structures, and systems

6—The Lovers—commitment, choice, balance, romance, partnership, spiritual path of love

7—The Chariot—forward motion, action, progressing on a path

8—Strength—compassion is strength, and you're stronger than you think

9—The Hermit—solitude is enlightening, isolation versus solitude, opportunities for focused learning, withdrawing

10—Wheel of Fortune—the hand of fate, find opportunities, learn to dance with the universe

11—Justice—justice is served/required, evaluate relationships/situations for fairness, boundaries, legal matters

12—The Hanged Man—surrender, limbo, sacrifice, eventual enlightenment

13—Death—ego death, change, endings, grief, renewal, liberation

14—Temperance—patience, balance, things take the time they take for a reason

15—The Devil—chained to the ego, bad habits/coping mechanisms, self-indulgence

16—The Tower—dramatic change in order to create a better present, burn it down to start again

17—The Star—hope; optimism; faith; dream big, kid

18—The Moon—intuition, deep emotions, mental health, spirituality, the subconscious

19—The Sun—happiness, action, expression, creativity, the arts

20—Judgment—rising up after death, redemption, liberation, discernment

21—The World—infinite paths; global connection; the end of one journey and the beginning of another; the world is your oyster, kid

The Minor Arcana

The Minor Arcana represent the more mundane details of our lives, like situations, people, temporary states, even though they might still feel very important to us. The Minor Arcana are split into the four elemental suits, and further categorized into the court cards versus the numerical Minor Arcana.

Suits

Swords are represented by the element of air, and they deal with thoughts, logic, mental health, learning, school, training, education, written communication, choices, cutting ties, confusion, and clarity. Some mnemonic devices for remembering swords and their element and associations are air head, sword of reason, the pen is mightier than the sword, clear cut.

Cups are represented by the element of water, and they deal with emotions, relationships (romantic, platonic, etc.), healing, intuition, spirituality, the subconscious, love, and connection. A few mnemonic devices for remembering cups and their element and associations are heart of the ocean, fill your own cup first, nourish others with your overflow, (e)motion of the ocean.

Wands (also called staffs, staves, or sticks) are represented by the element of fire, and they deal with communication, passion, drive, manifesting, action, collaboration, projects that may or may not be work related, and creativity. You can try mnemonic devices for remembering wands and their element and associations by thinking of the fiery sparks that fly out of a magic wand, wands manifest or make things happen, staffs or staves are like kindling for fire, and burning passion.

Pentacles (also called coins or discs) are represented by the element of earth, and they deal with money, abundance, stability, the work we do for a living, the home and hearth, material things, and health. Try mnemonic devices for remembering pentacles and their element and associations like buried treasure, fruits of your labor, fruits of the earth, nature's bounty, and salt of the earth.

The Royal Court

There is a royal court for each elemental suit, swords, cups, wands, and pentacles, and the court is made up of pages, knights, queens, and kings. The element of the suit influences the energy of the members of the royal court: for instance, the King of Pentacles would be a king in the realm of pentacles, so health, wealth, home, and hearth. Sometimes the court cards can represent you or aspects of you, and sometimes they represent someone in your life with those qualities. We don't think the gender of the card needs to refer to the gender of the person because gender is on a spectrum and people are who they are in beautiful and diverse ways that are beyond the binary. There are folks who are cisgender, gender fluid, nonbinary, trans, agender, and more. Even if you're a cisgendered woman, born biologically female and identifying as a woman, you could be represented by a knight, king, or page because those might be the experiences you're having in life. And there's no need to question your gender identity about it. That would be a separate thing. Likewise, if you're attracted to femmes in dating and you keep getting kings representing your love interest, that doesn't mean that you need to question your sexuality. Kings can be femmes too.

Many people struggle to remember all of the court cards and how to read them, so we created a guide to help you understand the energy of pages, knights, queens, and kings in general.

Pages, Princes, or Princesses have a very youthful, creative, playful, experimentative energy. They're just starting on their path. They're trying new approaches. The nature of the creative energy is determined by the suit. If the page is representing another person, they might be a child or younger person in the client's life.

Knights are on a quest, often rooted in spiritual, moral, or ethical values. Knights bring about change as well, like a new direction or movement toward a goal. The nature of that quest is determined by their suit: swords, cups, pentacles, or wands. It can also represent facing a challenge, or a battle, or courageously pursuing a path of purpose. If the knight is representing someone in the client's life, it could be a principled person or a mission, or someone still forging their way in life, or even someone who is challenging to them.

Queens are empowered leaders, whose own values and needs are important. Their self-care needs to be top-tier or the whole kingdom crumbles. They are in control of themselves and on their own path, and this is further colored by their suit. If a Queen is representing someone in the client's life, they could be a mature person who is nurturing or inspiring.

Kings are a mature energy, also empowered, and perhaps even leading or teaching others. There's a sense that they are at the top of the hierarchy so they are directly influencing others by necessity, whereas a Queen might just do that by choice. The suit determines how they influence others and where they are successful. If the King is representing someone in the client's life, it could be a person who is mature, sure of themselves, professional, experienced, and in control.

Like people, the royal court has their strengths and weaknesses, and the four suits, pentacles, wands, cups, or swords, add depth to what those strengths and weaknesses are. These are simplified explanations to help you understand the basic function of the member in the royal court, but there's more nuance to dive into through both study and intuition. Take some time with the imagery of whatever deck you're using and compare your intuition to the creator's interpretation.

The Aces

Aces represent new beginnings, paths, opportunities, and cycles, and they tend to bring in positive energy and urge you to take action.

Ace of Swords—sever ties with what is not serving you in order to move forward with focus. A new outlook or mentality. Freedom, and clarity of choice. Leave the past behind.

Ace of Cups—deep love and healing, restoration, regeneration within yourself. Self-love. New relationships or the deepening and healing of established relationships. A path of emotional and spiritual well-being.

Ace of Wands—an opportunity to follow your passions. Communication and creative energy. A new cycle of fulfilling work, projects, or personal connections. A spark.

Ace of Pentacles—new work opportunity, or opportunities for abundance that require your effort. A new home. New self-care or health regimen with concrete life changes.

A Rough-and-Ready Guide for Remembering the Minor Arcana

Outside of the court cards, all the Minor Arcana are associated with numbers. Since this is just an introduction, we're giving you an easy way to help remember the fifty-six Minor Arcana by remembering what the numbers represent and applying those meanings to the corresponding suit. For instance, the Two of Cups and the Two of Swords both conjure meanings of being paired and balanced, but because of the differences in their suits, the Two of Cups suggests love, harmony, and partnership, whereas the Two of Swords represents two forces in equal opposition or a stalemate. When you're gaining expertise and practicing by reading for others, it helps if you can have a rough-and-ready guide to numbers at the top of your head, and soon the meanings will become second nature.

- Two represents balance, partnership, harmony, and duality

- Three represents community, connection, friendship, and collaboration

- Four represents stability and/or stillness

- Five represents loss or instability/stress

- Six represents success, growth, recovery

- Seven represents instability that requires work that will pay off

- Eight represents regaining boundaries, awareness, and strength

- Nine represents integration, learning, wishes/fears, near-completion

- Ten represents the end of a cycle, completion, fullness, saturation

The Art of Reading for Yourself

The art of reading for yourself is born of consistency and experimentation. To start, find a nice space to work and set your environment however you prefer. Clear your mind as best you can using breathing techniques, and set an intention to be open to spiritual direction. Ask for what you need from your deity/guides/universe/deck, or whatever suits you, to guide you with clarity.

How Often Should You Read for Yourself or Get Readings?

We encourage reading often or daily to practice if you're learning, hoping to become professional, or are professional. Not everyone wants to read for themselves daily, though, and sometimes folks ask us how often they should get readings from professionals or friends. Here are some reading schedules that some people enjoy.

- Weekly, Moon Phase, or Monthly Forecast—if daily feels like a lot, some people like a tarot forecast for the week, moon phase, or month ahead.

- Seasonal/Holiday Readings—some people like to read around their major holidays or seasons to help them decide where to focus their energies for that part of the year. Some do just solstices and/or equinoxes.

- Event-Based—Something wild happening? Feeling confused? Ready for a life change? Get a reading!

- Annual—some people love just one reading a year, maybe around their birthday, or whatever date signifies a new year for them.

A Daily Practice

We highly recommend drawing a card every day to get to know the tarot better and to receive daily guidance from your deck. You can meditate on its meaning and message for a few minutes every morning. Better yet, journal a little about the card and what you think it means for you in the morning, and then check in again at night and journal about what you learned. We are all about testing your knowledge and checking up on your results. It can be helpful to ask a specific question to the cards so you get used to the way they communicate with you. You can ask whatever you like in a daily reading, but we have some suggestions for you:

- What do I need to know today?

- What do I need to embody?

- What will guide me today?

- What do I need to learn today?

- What will give me strength today?

- What can I let go today?

How to Ask Questions

If you're just starting out, start light. Even seasoned readers struggle to read for themselves about sensitive topics that they're very emotionally invested in. If there's something pressing that you want to read about but it's too hard for you to be objective and get clarity, you can ask a professional reader or talented friend to do the hard work for you. Seeing how others read is a great way to learn too. For your own readings for yourself though, ask open-ended questions. Avoid yes or no questions initially because tarot tends to be more nuanced than that. For example, asking a question like "Will I ever get married?" is too dependent on too many factors and choices that you and others would navigate. Instead, a more helpful question might be "What do I need to know about my love life right now?" or "How can I approach dating so I can find my life partner?"

It's also helpful to ask questions that are meant to help you along your healing journey, spiritual path, purpose, or whatever feels like it would provide you life guidance. Sometimes the specific things we want or worry about are more transient than we realize. What seems important now might not be next week due to totally unforeseen circumstances. It's okay to ask specific questions about events in the near future, but ask some big picture questions too. Be sure to balance questions about the mundane, or day-to-day, with questions of healing and spirituality. Tarot helps you become more self-aware, so well-rounded inquiries are essential.

Example Questions

- What do my guides want me to know?

- What is blocking me?

- What is supporting me?

- What am I afraid of?

- Where should I direct my energy?

- What do I need to understand?

- What should I focus on right now?

- What can I release?

- What is my strength?

- How can I approach X for success?

- How can I be of service?

- How am I growing?

- What is the nature of this situation?

- What is X embodying?

- What is the conflict?

- What is the solution?

Tarot and Dreams

Dreams are such an important part of spiritual and psychic work for many Roma, and tarot is a very useful tool for understanding the symbols and scenarios that arise in dreams. You may notice overlap between dream symbols and tarot symbols, and you can use tarot spreads to ask open-ended questions about aspects of a dream, a dream's overall message, action you should take, and more.

Also, when certain cards come up in your regular readings, they may be urging you to work more consciously with dreams.

Cards That We Associate with Dreamwork

- The Moon (dreams, subconscious, psychism)

- The High Priestess (mastering dreams, healing, subconscious work, psychism)

- The Queen of Cups (mastering emotional healing, relationships with others and yourself/your younger self, psychism, dreams)

- The Ace of Cups (new opportunities for healing, paying attention to dreams and psychism)

- The Hermit (self-reflection, meditation, dreamwork)

- The Hierophant (channeling information from deity/guides/the universe)

- The Nine of Swords and the Ten of Swords (nightmares that help you work through fears)

Helpful Tarot Questions for Dreamwork

- What does this symbol represent?

- What is this guide communicating to me?

- How can I embody this symbol?

- What is the obstacle?

- What is this obstacle teaching me?

- How can I approach healing this?

- What do I need to release?

- What is my strength?

- What wisdom is this dream sharing?

- What is asking for my attention right now?

- What is at the heart of the mystery?

- What is the advice for me?

- Where do I need to be gentle with myself?

- What kind of action do I need to take?

- Where do I need more understanding?

- What do I need to know?

- Where are my opportunities?

- How can I connect with my guides?

- What are my guides communicating in this dream?

- What is the fear holding me back?

- How is this fear serving me?

- How can I release this fear?

- What is my north star? (your guiding light)

- What is the change that I need to embrace?

- What is transforming in me?

- How can I support myself through this transformation?

Examples of Tarot Spreads for Dreams

Card 1: What's the situation? Card 2: What's the obstacle? Card 3: What's the solution?

Card 1: What is coming up to be healed? Card 2: How can I support myself through this? Card 3: What can I release?

Card 1: What is the message for my body? Card 2: What is the message for my mind? Card 3: What is the message for my heart? Card 4: What is the message for my spirit?

Card 1: What is the conscious issue? Card 2: What is the subconscious issue? Card 3: How can I approach integration?

Reading Tarot for Others

If you're just starting to read for others, then start small. Help the person find the right open-ended question, and pull no more than three cards so you can keep the messages clear and so you're not looking up card meanings forever. Treat a reading like a conversation—say what you understand the cards to mean, and ask if the person can relate to any aspects of what you know. Practice opening your senses and coming to your own interpretations intuitively first.

Consider the images in the card, and treat it like a dream or artwork you're analyzing, except you're finding personal connections. Only after you've done your own sensing and exploring, look up the meanings together. Don't make any hard-and-fast predictions if you're not sure about them. It's okay to be honest about what's confusing. Things can change, and we all have free will anyway, so sometimes the path isn't totally clear. Having a conversation with the person who volunteered for this practice reading will help you navigate anything that is cloudy, and you'll learn more in the process.

Three-Card Tarot Spreads

A three-card spread, which is usually three cards read from left to right, can be used for almost any situation, and you can use them for yourself or for others. There are some classics out there, and you can also make up your own. These are some of our favorites:

1. Past, 2. Present, 3. Future

1. Situation, 2. Obstacle, 3. Solution

1. Yourself, 2. The Other Person, 3. Your Connection

1. You, 2. The Situation, 3. The Advice

1. The Situation, 2. Action, 3. Perspective

1. Body, 2. Mind, and 3. Spirit (or Physical, Emotional, Spiritual)

A Relationship with the Cards

The cards represent humanity; whether they are parts of us, people in our lives, themes that characterize the human experience, or archetypes that humans create and play out, tarot is all of it. The more you practice, the more of a relationship you create with your deck. You get to know its tone, personality, quirks, and preferences. Whether you use tarot as a tool to channel divine wisdom or your own higher self, or if you think of tarot as a magical system itself, or both, taking the time to get to know your favorite deck(s) will serve you better than any one guide.

CHAPTER 6

The Basics of Tea-Leaf and Coffee Reading

You boil the water and select the herbs for your client, breathing in their sweet, green fragrance. Your teapot is an heirloom, and the dainty cup sits sweetly in its saucer. After preparing the tea ritually, you bring the tea tray out to the client and make a show of pouring the tea and the cascade of tea leaves into the cup. Steam rises, and you tell them to focus on what they wish to know.

Also known as tasseography, tassology, and tasseology, tasseomancy is the divinatory practice of reading the tea leaves, coffee grounds, or wine sediments in cups. There is often a ritual or ceremony of some kind that contextualizes the practice, even if it is very simple. Many cultures, mostly Asian, Middle Eastern, and North African, practice tasseomancy, and the symbols and their meanings can vary from culture to culture. The tea and coffee trade, which was rife with exploitation and colonizer violence, made tea and coffee popular all over the world. While many cultures practice different variations of tasseomancy, Roma are responsible for sharing the practice far and wide. Like palmistry and cartomancy, Romani-style tasseomancy became trendy wherever Roma traveled. In the 1920s and 1930s, Gypsy tea rooms sprang up all over cities, capitalizing on the exotic image of the Gypsy tea-leaf reader, even though anti-fortune-telling laws made it difficult for actual

Roma to practice the trade. This divinatory art is less popular now, but all the more reason to learn something special that not everyone can do.

We will share some of the most prominent symbolism passed down through our families, but because we know our readers come to this book with diverse backgrounds, we will mostly be teaching you how to interpret symbols for yourself. We will also share the preparation of tea and coffee, the suggested ritual for a reading, and some suggestions for tea and coffee blends. We're not the voice of authority for all Romani tasseomancy, but we are happy to share our thoughts. We encourage you to think of this as a taster of the art, and explore and learn from other readers too.

Jezmina's Tea-Leaf Reading Story

My grandmother started teaching me tea-leaf reading more formally when I was a preteen, the same way she was taught by her grandparents. My grandmother would come over to my parents' house for breakfast on Sunday mornings, and we usually had my Auntie Zina living with us, and sometimes an uncle. We would make crepes (also called blini) with fruit and sour cream, or yogurt and whipped cream, and have tea or coffee. We would eat, drink, and check in about our week, and when we finished, we exchanged cups. Even though my mother and auntie didn't read professionally, they both knew how to read and were very intuitive, and always taught me a lot. My grandmother was the final word, though.

Reading each other's cups was an opportunity for us to go deeper into each other's lives, and offer advice that we channeled from the ancestors, spirits, angels, or God, based on the symbols we saw. Rather than telling each other what to do, we used it as an opportunity to have meaningful conversations about our struggles and our goals, using the symbols as the key to unlocking those deep truths. I was learning our trade, but I was also learning how to talk directly with my loved ones about the important things. Roma don't do small talk, after all.

Paulina's Tasseography Story

The elders in my family always pushed me to learn everything I could about divination from any and all sources. Any book, article, from any resource was pushed on me. My family practiced tarot, palm, face, and trinket readings regularly, but only dabbled in tea and coffee readings. During times we were traveling or living in shops, we didn't always have a coffee maker, for economic reasons. We would usually make coffee in a pot on a burner, similar to Turkish coffee, but with a struggling American Gypsy family twist. As time went on, when we did have a coffee maker, the elders preferred it be made on the stove anyway. It was a little bit of a pain in the ass, but it is what it is.

One day, while going through the stacks of books my mom collected over the years, I brought up a book about tasseography. Knowing my family has strong roots in Turkey, I found parallels in our coffee-making habits. My grandmother said we used to practice coffee and tea readings but not so much anymore. She wanted me to read more about it and also use the cool new thing called the internet. I found myself teaching her things I learned, and over time the whole family joined in on the conversations. The hype died down and I didn't professionally perform Turkish coffee readings until I opened my own store in my early twenties, but it's now one of my favorite forms of divination. People get really excited when they hear that it's an option. I love the uniqueness, the flashback I get from making coffee on a burner, the whole ritual, and even the look on the client's face when they take the first sip. Many symbols draw parallels with symbols in astrology, tarot, and dream interpretation, so learning and relearning were a breeze.

The Plants Themselves

Both tea-leaf and coffee-ground reading are very old and find their origins in the discovery of the plants that make these divinatory methods possible. In animistic cultures like ours, it's also important to make sure that you have a kind and respectful connection with the plants and the tools that you work with for divination. Since you'll be deepening your relationship with the plants, it helps to know a little about their history first.

A Very Brief History of Coffee

Evidence suggests that coffee was first discovered in the 11th century in present-day Ethiopia by the nomadic Oromo people, the first group to cultivate the coffee plant. Coffee cultivation spread through trade to the Arabian Peninsula, and coffeehouses sprang up throughout North Africa and the Middle East. These coffeehouses were places of learning, discussion, and community connection. Trade and European colonization introduced coffee to Europe in the 1600s, and café culture developed in the 1700s. European colonizers spread coffee plantations throughout the Caribbean and South and Central America, fueled by the labor of enslaved and exploited Africans and Indigenous people.

A Very Brief History of Tea

Legend says that circa 2737 BCE, Emperor Shen Nong, the divine farmer, was drinking boiled water under a tree when tea leaves blew into his cup. First, powdered matcha was the tea of choice in China, but over time, loose-leaf tea became popular as well. Ritual developed around tea and tea drinking, as well as tea art. Tea arrived next in Japan in the 6th century CE and was consumed by the religious elite. Their own ceremonies and rituals evolved as well. China initially prospered by trading tea with the Dutch in the 1600s, and then the British. In an effort to avoid paying for tea, the British tried to trade opium instead, which quickly had devastating effects on China. When the Chinese refused to continue this trade, the Opium Wars (1839-1842 and 1856-1860) commenced. British colonizers also snuck tea seeds into India and began growing there to break the Chinese monopoly on tea, and those plantations were extremely exploitative of Indian workers.

Why the History of Coffee and Tea Matters

The violent history of tea and coffee is not over, and the effects of colonization continue in a number of harmful ways. Workers in South and Central America, Africa, Asia, and elsewhere are still exploited by European and North American companies. Growers are severely underpaid, mistreated, indentured, or actually enslaved. It's important to know where your tea and coffee come from. As much as you can, support companies with fair labor practices, and look for BIPOC-owned businesses.

Can I Read My Own Cup?

Absolutely, we think, but not everyone would agree. According to Jezmina's grandma, **no,** because "Your fears and hopes distort your reading." But Jez does it anyway. Please don't tell Grandma. She would be so mad. It really depends on your personality and your ability to distinguish between intuition and anxiety. We view readings for ourselves as journaling/introspective/self-discovery tools rather than a tool to predict the future exactly, though we do sometimes want divine advice for what lies ahead. We think Jezmina's grandma might be okay with this method, but honestly we were always too scared to ask. Reading for yourself can be a great way to learn. Just try not to take yourself too seriously as you're learning. Instead, use it as an intuitive exercise, keeping an eye out for the symbols you discover in dreams, art, and other experiences.

Setting an Intention before You Start

The magic of tasseomancy starts right before you prepare the tea or coffee with a blessing or intention. Once you have collected your materials, consider what your goals are for your reading and whom/what you want to call on for protection and assistance. Some things to keep in mind when coming up with your intention/blessing:

- Whom are you reading for?

- What do you wish for them/yourself?

- Who/what protects you while you open yourself up to messages?

- Where do you believe you get your messages, or who or what facilitates it?

What an Intention/Blessing Might Look Like for Reading Yourself

Ancestors/deities/guides/universe (whomever/whatever you address), please bless and protect me as I read for myself. Help me set aside my ego, my hopes, and my fears, and read with clarity, wisdom, compassion, and understanding. Assist me with _____ (if you have a specific question), and guide me to the best path for my best self. Thank you for your love, protection, and assistance.

What an Intention/Blessing Might Look Like for Someone You're Reading

Ancestors/deities/guides/universe (whomever/whatever you address), please bless and protect me as I read for _____. Help me set aside my ego, my hopes, and my fears, and read with clarity, wisdom, compassion, and understanding. Help me connect with their ancestors/deities/energy to receive what they need to know to guide them along their best path for their best self. Help me communicate what they need to know in a way that they can understand and accept these messages. Help me assist them with _____ (if they have a specific question). Thank you for your love, protection, and assistance.

Drinking with Intention

If you're drinking by yourself, turn it into a meditation. Breathe deeply, open your mind, focus on your intention/blessing, and mentally ask any of the questions you have. If you're drinking with another person/other people, enjoy your conversation, and make sure that the conversation is warm. You can talk about what is going on in your life, and what you want to know about from the cup, or really anything else that feels appropriate. This is a time to bond and set the energy right.

Questions We Get

We are diving into the preparation of coffee and tea for the purposes of divination. We'll start with the questions people love to ask when we teach tasseomancy:

Q: Can I use milk or cream in my tea or coffee?

A: It messes up the texture of the grounds or leaves and makes them hard to read. Milk, or its alternatives, you can almost get away with, but it's not great. Cream is a clumpy disaster. Just letting you know.

Q: Can I use sweetener?

A: Sure!

Q: Can I blow on my tea or coffee?

A: Of course. Just treat it like any other beverage.

Q: Can I put an ice cube in it to cool it down?

A: Absolutely.

Q: What if I can't drink it all? Can I pour some out?

A: It's just a cup. You can drink it all. Just drink it. You're supposed to drink it.

Q: What kind of cup should I use?

A: Ideally, use a shallow, round-bottomed cup with either white or another light color inside, and ideally no pattern inside the cup, or very little pattern. This is just the easiest to read. Mugs or deep cups with perpendicular angles can catch too many leaves or coffee grounds. It's difficult to see the dregs against dark colors or elaborate patterns as well. Classic bone china style tea and coffee cups are ideal. You can find them at thrift shops and antique stores or buy them new.

Coffee Ritual

Coffee reading is more popular in Eastern Europe and throughout North Africa, West Asia, and East Asia. However, Roma from any group might read coffee for any number of reasons, from personal preference to influence from friends or family. Coffee reading itself is a little messier and darker because the grounds spread out all over the cup, and you can even read the saucer for additional messages. It has its own distinct aesthetic that adds to the experience.

Materials

- A *cezve*, which is a small copper coffeepot with a long handle and a lip on the rim. We recommend Romani-made copperware by Brateiu Traditional Handmade Copper Art from Romania. You can order from their Facebook page and it's the best you can get.

- Very finely ground coffee, like Kurukahveci Mehmet Efendi Turkish coffee

- Water

- Sugar (optional)

- A burner on your stove (gas flame is ideal)

- Small cups for serving

- Saucers

- Spoons

Method

- Once you've gathered your materials, set an intention/invoke a blessing.

- Add one spoonful of coffee to the coffeepot per cup of coffee.

- Add sugar to taste (typical ratio is 1:1).

- Stir the sugar and coffee together very well. This is also the time to stir in any spices if using.

- Use the coffee cup to measure the water for the coffee, and add the water. This should create a foam on top in the coffeepot.

- Mix together well without losing too much of the foam. You will not mix the coffee at all after this point.

- Hold the coffeepot over a low flame from the stove just so that it simmers.

- The coffee should begin to foam at the sides. This is great. Let it build a nice foam, but not so much that it runs over.

- Take the coffee off the flame, and divide the foam equally among cups with a spoon.

- Slowly pour the coffee into the cups, being careful not to ruin the foam.

- Serve.

Spices You Might Want to Use

You don't need to add spices, but you can if you want. You could use anything to add a little kick and extra magic to your cup, but here are some common ones with their spiritual properties.

- Allspice—money, luck, healing
- Black Pepper—protection
- Cacao—healing, heart opening, creativity
- Cardamom—balance, clarity, joy
- Chili—protection, power, creativity, passion
- Cinnamon—love, prosperity
- Clove—love, passion, fidelity, abundance
- Ginger—prosperity, abundance, energy
- Nutmeg—luck, wishes, abundance
- Vanilla—love (platonic, spiritual, romantic), beauty, healing

Drinking the Coffee

Allow the sediment of the fine grounds to sink to the bottom of the cup. Drink as much of the liquid as you can. Clamp your lips tight at the rim to strain out the grounds when you're running low on coffee because it's gross to get a mouthful of grounds, even if the coffee is delicious. It can be helpful to rotate the cup as you're sipping at this stage so the grounds don't all run to one side of the cup.

When you've drunk all the coffee:

- Swirl the grounds three times.

- Turn the coffee cup upside down on its saucer to let it drain.

- Rotate the cup while it's upside down three times so that the handle returns to where it began thrice.

- Wait a few minutes for all the liquid to drain before reading.

- You can also read what's in the saucer for any closing messages.

Tea Ritual

Tea-leaf reading is popular all over, and the style varies all over, ranging from the type of tea to how it is served. What you get in a tea bag is cut far too small to read, or even drink loose comfortably because it all ends up in your mouth, so make sure you buy "loose-leaf tea." Here are some common teas that you can read with, based on your preference.

- Black Tea—more traditional, usually a finer cut, and the easiest for most people to read because the smaller leaves create more distinct symbols. Orange pekoe refers to the cut of the leaf—it's Jezmina's grandmother's preferred leaf to use because it's small, but not too small.

- Green Tea—bigger leaves, a little "messier," more like reading an inkblot, which can be fun if you like that!

- Red Tea—looks more like tiny sticks in the loose form.

- Herbal Tea—often includes flowers and varied textures, which for some people is distracting, but for others is very helpful.

Herbal Blends to Consider

If you're drinking herbal tea, you can use any herbs or blend of herbs that you want, whether they're premade or mixed by you. We have a list of a few herbs you might like to try, and the spiritual qualities that they can bring to your cup.

- Blue Lotus—psychism, dreams
- Calendula—healing, tranquility, luck
- Chamomile—healing, happiness, tranquility
- Hyssop—protection, purity
- Lavender—protection, purity, tranquility
- Lemon—it's a fruit, but it's lucky and protective
- Mugwort—psychism, dreams
- Oat Straw—healing, happiness
- Red Clover—success, luck, money
- Rose—healing, love (spiritual, romantic, platonic), beauty

Materials

- Tea leaves of your choice (more about this later)
- Teapot without a strainer in the spout (if it's only you, you could just use a cup)
- Teacup and saucer
- Kettle
- Spoon
- Sugar or sweetener of your choice (optional)

Method

- Gather your materials and set your intention/blessing.
- Boil enough water in the kettle.
- Scald/bless the pot by pouring some freshly boiled water into the teapot, swirling it three times, and then pouring it out in the sink through the spout.

- Add your tea leaves to the empty, blessed teapot, 1 spoonful per cup.

- Fill the teapot with the boiled water.

- Let steep for the appropriate time depending on the type of tea.

- Swirl the tea around in the pot so the leaves rise.

- Pour the tea into cups. (If there aren't enough leaves, you can spoon some out into the cup.)

- Add whatever sweetener you like, if you're using it.

Drinking the Tea

Allow the tea leaves to sink to the bottom of the cup. Drink as much of the liquid as you can. Clamp your lips tight at the rim when you're running low on tea so you don't get too many tea leaves in your mouth, which is not particularly fun or mystical, although they won't do you any harm. It can be helpful to rotate the cup as you're sipping at this stage so the tea leaves don't all run to one side of the cup.

When you've drunk all the tea:

- Swirl the tea leaves three times clockwise or counterclockwise (up to your preference but it helps to be consistent).

- Turn the teacup upside down on its saucer to let it drain.

- Rotate the teacup while it's upside down three times so that the handle returns to where it began thrice.

- Wait a few minutes for all the liquid to drain before reading.

- There usually won't be leaves in the saucer for you to read like there is with coffee, but if there are, feel free to read them as a closing message.

Interpreting the Symbols

All of the symbols we're offering come with the caveat that depending on your experiences and cultural context, not all the interpretations might apply or ring true to you. We're giving you the traditional meanings just for information, but you are highly encouraged to create your own index or symbols and meanings based on what you resonate with. Also know that these symbols might mean something very different to the person you're reading, and you should take that into account as well. As we're writing this together, we're discovering that our families sometimes have different or even opposite interpretations of symbols, which we've noted, so even among Romani families there is variation.

It's a good idea for you to make your own lexicon of symbols so you can keep track of what different symbols mean to you. You can use our guide for inspiration, and there are plenty of symbol dictionaries out there to help you too. The important part is reflecting on your own meanings and how they evolve over time with experience and practice.

Animals

Animals have so many different cultural and personal associations that it's important to use your own interpretations. For instance, Roma see cats and dogs as helpful and traditionally would have them in camps because dogs would guard the kids and home, and cats would keep away the mice, so both of these animals are often read positively by Roma. However, for other Roma, they might have more of a negative interpretation—cats and dogs are sometimes seen as unclean because of their habits and might not always be welcome inside the house.

Our two families have differences in the way they read cats, though it doesn't have much to do with impurity. Jezmina's grandmother read cats as advice to be sly and cunning like a cat to get out of tricky situations. Paulina's family reads cats as a symbol of attraction, because cats are choosy about whom they go to, so they would be lucky in a love reading. In the same vein, Paulina's family would read snakes traditionally as enemies, but Jezmina's grandmother liked snakes, and while she acknowledged the traditional meaning is important, in her own cup she would see them as symbols of change and transformation because of the way they shed their skin. Jezmina's family tends to see mice as representing small losses because mice nibble away at your food, but Paulina's family sees mice as a lucky sign that good things are coming because it means your home is prosperous enough to attract a mouse. So, think about the qualities of the animal and the context that is important to you, and your associations with them, and take your interpretation from there.

Objects

Certain objects also have different meanings, depending on your cultural context and experience. So, for instance, a sword is usually seen as a threat, but if you're a tarot reader, you might associate it with the sword suit, a sign of a person's mental or intellectual life. Maybe you're a blacksmith, or on a fencing team. Or maybe you love swords and see them as empowering and protective. Even in this case, there is a reason that the person needs to feel empowered or protective, so, maybe some kind of threat is present, even if that threat is emotional rather than physical.

Even cultural associations change over time. Not everyone is looking to get married these days, so we don't always read a ring as representing marriage unless the person is directly asking about a committed relationship. Instead, we might read it as making an important commitment, personally or professionally. Or maybe it is not a ring, but a wheel representing forward motion, or a circle representing wholeness or completion. Perhaps it feels like the wheel of fortune, and it's about riding out the plans fate has in store for you the best you can. Ask the client questions and use your intuition.

Elements

- Air—might appear as part of a scene, like leaves blowing, clouds, a starry sky, etc. Air represents the mind, rationality, new beginnings, freedom.

- Earth—could appear as a mountain, a cliff, a field, stones. Earth represents stability, health, prosperity, strength, and groundedness.

- Fire—it might be small like a candle flame, or much bigger. Fire represents energy, what we do in the world, creativity, passion, anger, danger, destruction making way for creation.

- Water—might appear as waves, rain, an ocean, a lake, a river. Water often represents change, adaptability, psychism, deep emotions, healing, and purification. However, some families, like Paulina's, associate water with bad luck and accidents.

Numbers and Letters

You might see numbers or letters in the cup. Usually letters would refer to a person's name, and numbers refer to timing or amounts. So, if someone comes to you wondering about a new relationship, and you see a Y and a 3, it's worth investigating—does their name start with a Y? Depending on what else is in the cup, the 3 might suggest a timeline—like in three months they'll make a decision about the relationship. We try not to be too predictive in readings because people can so easily misunderstand, and it's important to empower people to make their own choices, but sometimes you'll get strong feelings and symbols, and it seems clear. Check in with the person you're reading though before going too far into their business.

Common Interpretations

Looking for symbols in a cup is like spotting shapes in the clouds. It won't look like an artist's representation, but it will look like something to you. Trust your intuition and go with your first thought. Try not to overthink it and keep changing your mind about what a symbol is. Go with your instinct and commit.

- Acorn—prosperity

- Arrows—going in the right direction, on the right path

- Bassinet—baby

- Bird—news is coming, and some families see this as good news, whereas others read birds as bad news

- Boat—a trip overseas

- Cat—cleverness, attraction, seduction, but for some they could represent untrustworthiness
- Clover—good luck
- Cow—prosperity
- Cross—trials
- Crown—success, money, promotion
- Cup—wishes fulfilled
- Diamond—money/prosperous marriage
- Dog—loyalty, fidelity, trust, companionship, and friendship
- Fire—passion and/or danger
- Fish—ease and good fortune/wisdom
- Flowers—good relationships/marriage, manifestation
- Fox—a sly enemy
- Goat—danger
- Hat—success
- Heart—love
- Horse—strength and good fortune
- Horseshoe—good luck
- House—new home
- Ladder/Staircase—travel
- Lightning—accident
- Moon—psychism, identity crises
- Mountain—triumph after a struggle
- Mouse—small losses, or good luck, depending on your family (seeing a mouse in your house means that you have abundance)
- Owl—death omen in Romani culture

- Pig—wealth

- Rabbit—quick results

- Ring—marriage

- Scales—justice, impending legal issue

- Scissors—an argument or breakup

- Sheep—prosperity

- Shoes—travel and work

- Skull—death, which can be a metaphorical death, like an ending

- Snake—you have an enemy

- Square—stability, money

- Star—success

- Sun—happiness

- Sword/Any Weapon—watch your back, conflict

- Trees—healing, prosperity, strength

- Triangle—wisdom, empowerment

- Water (waves)—purification, or bad luck and accidents

- Wolf—a spirit is visiting you, such as an ancestor, angel, or spirit guide

Scenes

Once you've identified some symbols, start to build a scene. How do all of these symbols connect? Rotate the cup, look at it from different angles, soften your gaze, look at it from a distance, look at it up close. All the information you pick up is valuable—you're putting together a narrative of some sort. What does the mood of the cup feel like? Are there tea leaves or grounds everywhere that make it feel chaotic? Or does the cup look clean and peaceful? The mood of the cup gives you the tone of the reading. If you're having trouble getting the whole idea, share what you see with the person and ask if it makes sense. Have a conversation. This is how you learn. If you're reading for yourself and it doesn't make sense, journal about what you see and write down your associations. See if it makes sense later.

Parts of the Cup and Timing

Some readers split the cups into many segments to determine a timeline of events. Jezmina's grandmother believed that symbols at the bottom of the cup are the most present and pressing, and where they are further toward the rim represents how far they are in the future.

Some readers, like Paulina's family, establish timing by the handle instead. The handle represents the present, and then moving counterclockwise, the events unfold into the future. Whatever is right below the handle represents the past.

According to Jezmina's grandma, tiny flecks of leaves or grounds at the top of the cup represent good luck birds, which bear good news (though Paulina's family doesn't read this way). If you have a lot of little bird flecks near the rim, they take the sting out of any unlucky symbols elsewhere in the cup. You can decide what you believe here.

Our Last Sip

Tasseomancy is a beautiful divinatory practice and we could say much more on it, but for the purposes of our book, we will leave you with the advice that the more you practice this art, the better you get at it. One of our favorite things about reading the cup is how conversational it is. It's time for you to get to know yourself, your family, friends, loved ones, or clients better. We recommend that as you are learning, you make it a social event with the people around you. It's a fun way to connect, and also refine your own lexicon of symbols and meanings, and your ability to interpret them.

CHAPTER 7

Advanced Fortune-Telling Techniques

Admittedly, "advanced" is a relative concept. What might be advanced for one person could feel like beginner level for someone else, and vice versa. Some practices seem deceptively simple to do, but in actuality take a lot of practice and dedication to actually master. So keep an open mind about what we are calling advanced.

Pay attention to symbols that recur in your dreams, and special signs that come to you when you're going about your daily life, as well as what comes up during divination sessions. Signs and omens have their own ways of revealing themselves through multiple channels. You can't force it.

Flame Reading

You begin with candle gazing, as outlined in Chapter 2: How to Strengthen Your Intuition, by sitting in meditation to purify your mind and awaken your third eye. You might do flame reading if you are working a spell with candle magic, and you can observe how the candle burns to see how the spell will play out. Or you can just read the flame for purely divinatory purposes and use it as a tool to ask questions. You can do this with a camp-fire as well, but we imagine that most of our readers will be using candles.

These are some possible interpretations, but you can develop your own over time and with practice.

- Flame leaning to the right: yes

- Flame leaning to the left: no

- Flame sputtering: it's a struggle and there are forces working against you

- Flame going out on its own for no reason: there is an evil eye on you and interfering with your work

- Flame growing tall and burning bright: you are particularly blessed in your endeavors

- Flame suddenly engulfing the candle and burning out of control: the evil eye is on you and you need to cleanse

- Flame with a color at the center: depending on the color, it indicates a type of blessing: green for abundance, blue for happiness, and black for protection

- Flame with white smoke: your wishes are heard

- Flame with black smoke: your plans will not come to pass and cleansing is required

- A candle burning with a lot of wax dripping like tears means crying and sorrow, but it's good to process those emotions

You can also read the melted wax that pools in and around the candleholder after the candles have burned down the same way you would read tea leaves or coffee grounds in the cup or saucer. The symbols that remain are messages to give you more information about your spell, question, or intention.

Pendulum Reading

Tarot can be finicky with yes-or-no questions because the nature of tarot is symbolic, nuanced, and complex. Open-ended questions are usually better for tarot. Tea-leaf and coffee reading is also heavily symbolic, and while it can give yes-or-no answers, it doesn't always. And palmistry is more rooted in your personality traits and nature, and the broad strokes of your life. All of these are wonderful tools; however, there might be times when a simple yes or no will do. Some readers will still use tarot for this, but we prefer to use a pendulum for yes-or-no questions.

This is one of those deceptively simple practices, because the physical action of working with a pendulum is very straightforward. Anyone can do it. But to be good at it, you need a lot of psychic discipline, and you need to be very open to the divine or universal source you are connecting with. It's a little too easy to influence the pendulum yourself to get the answers you want without realizing it, so doing this well requires being on top of your game cleansing, protecting, and centering yourself daily.

Pendulum divination dates back to ancient Egypt, Greece, and Rome. Pendulums may be made of glass, metal, wood, stone, or crystal, which is attached to a cord or chain. You can also use any necklace instead of a pendulum, as our families did. If you don't need to buy something special to do it right, why spend money, right? But pendulums are beautiful, so they are nice to have if you want one. Find a pendulum (or necklace) you resonate with and bless it in your practice, with smoke, oil, moonlight, sunlight, or water (unless the stone is not water-safe). You can even just hold the pendulum and tell it what your intentions are for working with it.

How to Use a Pendulum

- Address the spirits/deities you will be working with while you hold the pendulum by the top of its chain or cord so that it is perfectly still. Be sure you're not subtly moving it yourself.

- Ask the pendulum to show you what yes looks like (usually clockwise circle) and what no looks like (usually counterclockwise circle).

- Ask your yes-or-no question.

- Stay still and focused as you allow the pendulum to answer you through your ancestors, spirit guides, angels, deities, higher self, or whoever.

- A small or big circle indicates a small or big "yes-or-no."
- A side-to-side motion means "maybe." Sometimes we're not ready to know, or the answer has not been decided.

Scrying

Scrying is popular across many cultures, and simply means seeing. You can scry simply by gazing at an object or substance and entering a meditative state, which allows your mind's eye to see beyond what is there and find the symbols that appear. You can scry using a campfire or candle flame, water in a black bowl, drops of ink in water, smoke, a crystal ball, a black mirror, obsidian, clouds in the sky . . . the list goes on. Don't get frustrated or discouraged if you don't see anything right away, or if what you see doesn't immediately make sense. This is one of the more challenging methods for many, and these divinatory arts take time to master—that's why it's called a practice.

There are many benefits to scrying because it forces you to flex your psychic muscles and fine-tune your ability to see or intuit in any situation. It is also a great meditation practice in and of itself. It's very helpful to try out different scrying tools that you like in order to understand your gifts and preferences better. Do you prefer working with water, air, fire, or earth? Or all four? You'll find out! And a regular scrying practice will help you learn to trust your vision and interpret your own symbols with more confidence over time.

Trinket and Charm Reading

Trinket and charm casting is wonderful for new learners and experts alike because you collect your own small objects, charms, and trinkets, and use them as your divinatory tools. That way, you know exactly what the objects mean to you, but as you continue to cast with them, your understanding of the meaning deepens. Trinket casting also helps you develop your understanding of spatial relationships between objects and what that means, and this is helpful for reading cards, palms, tea leaves or coffee grounds, almost anything.

We include here an excerpt from a prose poem "Lucy the Dukkerer" by Raine Geoghegan from her poetry collection, *The Talking Stick: O*

Pookering Kosh, about a relative in her extended family who read charms on Epsom Downs in England. Raine's poetry is a beautiful example of Romani storytelling and cultural preservation.

. . . Her long hair is plaited and tied up on top of her head; it hasn't been cut in years. She's smoking her pipe just like her mother used to. She unwraps the dusty charms from an old cloth that she keeps in a deep pocket and places them in her red felt hat which lies upturned on the grass. A customer has come over and is now kneeling in front of her, fidgeting and yawning. Lucy takes the money, picks up the hat, shakes it hard then beckons for the woman to take one of the charms. This is done three times, the first represents the past, the second, the future, the third the present. Each charm is turned over carefully in her hand before placing it on the bright red square of muslin that is on the blanket. She uses all sorts of charms to tell people's futures, tiny horseshoes, coins, crystals and even a variety of coloured buttons. "The yoks tells me everythin." Lucy knows that the charms are just something to concentrate on. "After all, I can't sit and dikk at someone's face for too long, can I?"

How to Select Your Trinkets and Charms

Anything can be a trinket that you cast with, a button, brooch, a broken earring, a coin, a seed, bone, tooth, marble, stone, ring, bracelet charm, small toy. . . . For ease of casting, they should be small enough that you can cast them all at once from your hands or a small bag like you're casting dice for a game to see what numbers you get. (You can also read with dice).

Select whatever you're drawn to collecting or that you serendipitously find. Take your time selecting between nine to thirteen items (or more or less). Let them reveal themselves to you over time. You don't have to rush out and buy a bunch of trinkets. They should feel meaningful to you.

Select a diverse array of objects that can cover different themes and archetypes, and that you can easily assign different meanings to.

Assigning Your Trinkets Meaning

Look for inspiration in all places and directions. Trinkets can have complex meanings or simple ones. Consider what you associate with the object; for instance, a key unlocks doors, so maybe it would represent opportunity. Or, since keys also lock doors, it could represent secrets. It depends on what you feel most strongly when you work with the object. A feather might represent communication, a heart charm could represent love, a bone could represent death/endings, and a thimble could be hard work, skill, or even protection. It's up to you.

Keep in mind how the object came into your possession. For instance, an heirloom ring passed down the generations could represent marriage, but also ancestors, commitment, family, or legacy. Consider the object's origins too. Maybe you found an acorn in your garden. An acorn is a seed and could represent abundance but also your personal connection to the natural world. Maybe you found it in your best friend's garden, and so it also has come to represent friendship and growth.

Ylvadroma Marzanna Radziszewski, aka Bimbo Yaga, suggests:

> Look through your home, altar and collections for items that stand out to you. You can add trinkets and replace others as often as you need until your collection feels complete, functional, purposeful. I have a very large trinket collection that I've been building for the better part of thirty years and a few times a year I bring all my trinkets together and reset my trinket reading set, adding new pieces with new stories to fill in the gaps and add new perspectives to the stories my trinket reading set tells as well as swapping pieces to better reflect and embody the stories already represented in my trinket reading set.

Ylva also makes some suggestions for signifiers to have represented in your trinket collection; just to get your creative juices flowing:

> Loyalty—helps to assess fealty in relationships
> Teacher—identify where learning, mentorship, or guidance is needed or available from or for querent

Secrets—identify if information needs to be shared, withheld

Timing—offer perspective around when to take action

Travel—can help identify when someone might need to make movement in their life

Communication—can represent negotiations, contracts, conversation

Ancestors—use to connect with ancestors (of family, blood, community, spirit, etc.)

Guiding Spirits—can indicate a need to call upon or tend those relationships

Innovation—get creative, a new idea or inspiration is needed

Heartbreak—are there old grievances, emotions, betrayals coming up for air and attention

Altar—bitch, you need to take a beat and regroup. Go to your altar or anywhere you find your center

Shadow—things you may be running from that need to be acknowledged

Let it go—we all carry hope for different outcomes, but this ain't it

Casting

You can hold the objects in your hands or in a bag and set an intention. That can be a question, a theme, or a request for guidance. When you're ready, loose the trinkets on the surface you're reading on like you're casting dice. You might cast trinkets on a table or a cloth, but many casters use a grid, whether imaginary or physical (usually painted on a cloth), to help read where the trinkets fall and how they relate to each other. You can make your own grid or purchase one. Notice where they fall, if any touch, what's in the center, what's furthest away, any patterns they create.

As an alternative, you can also cast charms the way Lucy does in Raine's poem by placing them all in a hat and asking a client to draw three: the first one represents the past, the second the present, and the third the future. This is how Paulina's family does trinket reading too.

Grids and Spreads

You are welcome to make up your own grid or spread for trinket reading, or you can also use the following spread from Ylvadroma Marzanna Radziszewski, aka Bimbo Yaga, as a template to develop your own reading style.

Ylva's Perspective

This is a trinket reading for gaining clarity in regards to a specific inquiry, also suitable for general insight. You will need your trinkets and an altar space; you can also work with your cartomancy deck of choice if you wish. Set your container and clear your mind as best you can, focus on the purpose of this divination session, and spread your trinkets into a circle on the altar, leaving plenty of space in the center (at least two hands breadth.) When ready, draw six trinkets, one at a time, reflecting on the following intentions for their role as signifiers in this reading:

1. Heart—can provide clarity of what is at the heart of the matter, a way of understanding the nature of current circumstances.

2. Self—can provide insight into the nature of your relationship with self and how to approach your intrapersonal dynamics in regard to current circumstances.

3. Relationships—can provide guidance for how you approach others at this time, a way of focusing your attention on the people you choose to invite into your life.

4. Action—can provide suggestions or considerations for specific action steps or areas of your life that need to be addressed in regard to the current circumstances.

5. Community—can provide insight about your role in your larger community, workplace, and with people/circumstances you need to be in relationship with. Can also provide insight about things to look out for in regard to others.

6. Purpose—can provide insight into how to focus your work in the world at this time; can also offer insight as to how this current circumstance may be affecting you in regards to the bigger picture of your intentions for yourself.

CHAPTER 8

Spiritual and Personal Development Aspects of Fortune-Telling

For many Roma, fortune-telling in its most basic form is a respectable profession that puts food on the table and keeps people happy and coming back for more time with you. At its highest form, fortune-telling helps us do all of that and become better, more self-aware people, in tune with ourselves, each other, and the divine. Although fortune-telling is becoming more popular, it's still not a common profession, but you don't need to do it professionally to benefit spiritually. By engaging with the methods, even just by reading this book, you are already taking the first step towards spiritual development, so, congratulations! Keep up the good work.

Divination, when taken seriously, enriches you with new depth and vibrancy, and brings culture and spice into your life. fortune-telling practices span the globe, manifesting uniquely within each region. In Europe, tarot card reading, palmistry, and crystal gazing prevail, while Eastern cultures like China and Japan embrace astrology, *I Ching*, and feng shui. African communities rely on diviners, bone throwing, and dream interpretation, while the Middle East incorporates astrology and coffee ground reading. In the Americas, Indigenous tribes utilize sacred stones, smoke patterns, and elements' movements for divination. Pacific Islanders employ seers and natural elements like shells for insights. This is not a comprehensive list of all divination methods in all of these parts of the globe, but a sampling, and among all these regions there are further diversity, trade, and exchange. While some of these practices are unique to the groups that created them, each universally offers guidance, reflecting cultural beliefs and a profound connection between individuals and the mystical forces shaping their lives.

When practicing fortune-telling, be sure to educate yourself and stay aware of anything that may be cultural appropriation or infringing on closed practices. By honoring and respecting the origins of other practices, you are aiding in your growth in the most authentic way. And by developing your own intuition and rituals, you are adding your own threads to the web of interconnectedness with all beings.

Paulina on Personal Spiritual Development

Spirituality can transcend cultural and ethnic boundaries, and resonate globally across all societies. As a kid, I remember so many different people walking in the shop, especially when we did business in larger cities like San Francisco and Los Angeles, California. No matter the religion, skin color, ethnicity, or cultural background, our clients felt a level of comfort of familiarity in the shop. It's kind of like traveling to a different country where everything feels foreign, then, you spot your favorite fast food chain or café, and you can't help but make a quick pit stop for a little sense of grounding wherever you are. Because I got to meet so many people, I often heard different stories and developed different understandings of people, what they go through, and how they live. This exposure can cultivate gratitude for your own blessings and instill humility by recognizing the interconnectedness of everyone's journey. I believe I am changed after every encounter.

Jezmina on Personal Spiritual Development

As someone with a lot of fire in me, I push myself too hard. I love to be helpful, to be of service, to fix, connect, network, set up, heal, solve, and spin everything. I also have my own struggles to deal with, like a trauma history and chronic illness. I have learned the hard way several times over that I cannot do this job, or any other job, at my own expense, whether that's emotional, physical, or spiritual. In order to be of service, and be viable and consistent, I need to be taking care of myself threefold behind the scenes. I have had to learn to value myself because it is not something I was taught; I can't rely on others to do that for me.

I am responsible for reading my own energy, maintaining boundaries, saying yes or no, and generally making sure that I am nourished enough to hold space for other people and do spiritual work with them. In order to help others, I need to help myself. When I love myself, I am able to love others in a healthier way. Fortune-telling requires that I work on myself, and also that I allow the work to change me. I am always transforming, and I can't get too attached to who I used to be. Spiritual work, for me, is a balance between personal accountability and faith in the divine.

Being Growth-Oriented

Doing what you love creates a positive personal change, which ripples outward beyond yourself. The discipline and dedication needed to hone these skills are beneficial in themselves because the practices are meditative and grounding, and you're able to share what you learn with others as you master it. Aiding others through fortune-telling and divination is reciprocal; as you assist others, however different or similar to you they may seem, you inadvertently aid your own growth, creating a symbiotic cycle of self-improvement. When you are consistently preaching about spirituality, healing techniques, listening to your intuition, and holistic guidance, it's pretty difficult not to take your own advice . . . . you know the saying, you practice what you preach.

Ancestor Work

Everyone has ancestors. We all came from somewhere. A lot of traditions, including ours, involve maintaining relationships with your ancestors and beloved dead; however these practices vary even among Roma. Some Roma do not speak the names of their deceased in order not to disturb them, and others leave out offerings of food or drink so that they feel honored and considered. Ancestors are the deceased who came before you in your family, whether you knew them or not.

Beloved dead are anyone you love whom you have lost, whether you were related or not. Some people even count celebrities or cultural icons among their beloved dead, hence words like transcestors, meaning trans icons who have passed on and feel like revered elders or family for the trans community at large. You can build meaningful relationships with almost anyone on the other side if it's a genuine connection. The realms of the dead and of dreams are close in proximity, with some overlaps, so dreams are a good space to meet with your dead, as are readings, meditation, trance states, and more. You can have this kind of close familial relationship with any guides or deities you work with too, or animals, plants, elements, or if you prefer, you might connect with your wisest self this way.

If you're not sure who your ancestors are due to adoption, displacement, family drama, or other reasons, you can still reach out to them and have deep relationships if you want to. If this appeals to you, think of your ancestors like allies, speak to them lovingly, give them offerings, ask them to protect your dreams, and to guide you through your healing, and to help you on your path. In that same vein, if there are ancestors you would rather never work with, or at least not work with for right now, you can make that boundary and tell them to stay away from you. Our friend, Ylvadroma Marzanna Radziszewski, aka Bimbo Yaga, suggests sending any troubled ancestors you need space from to a deep ocean of ancestor spirits for continued healing. This can be especially helpful to do with any recently dead whom you're connected with and who have not yet processed their life on earth and are lingering uncomfortably close to you. You can have boundaries with the dead, just like you can with the living.

The benefits of working with ancestors are many. First, if you learn how to communicate with them, they can aid you in your divination work by giving you messages and hints throughout the readings. Aside from professional blessings ancestors can bestow upon you by sending you psychic information, ancestors help us know ourselves and where we come from. Everyone has both intergenerational trauma and blessings, but we're not always aware of or working on or with these energies. Ancestor work will bring you to the source of your generations-long poverty wound, or connect you with the line of mediumship that runs through your family like a river.

Ancestors and beloved dead, like living family and friends, love to give advice, and that can be very helpful. Even though they're spirits, they still have their own opinions, personalities, and biases, so they might contradict each other, or give you guidance that doesn't feel right for you sometimes. They might have a lot of wisdom, but they aren't gods. Take what they say with a grain of salt, though remember that they really can be helpful. For instance, Jezmina's grandmother, mother, auntie, and uncle have all passed on, and every time Jezmina asks for their ancestors' advice, Auntie Zina always pops up to tell Jez to get married again. That is very much reflective of what auntie believes is best, and not what Jezmina actually wants. But it makes Jezmina laugh every time.

You can use any of the divination tools we covered to connect with ancestors, even your own palm, and this works best when you specifically address your ancestors with the trinkets, tea, tarot, or whatever else you're using. However, these easy rituals and practices will help strengthen your connection to the dead so that connecting with them becomes easier and easier.

Ancestor Altar

Your altar is a place to feed and nourish relationships with ancestors and your beloved dead. You can go there to talk to them as you would any living person, and to listen to what they say back. You can set up your altar on a small table, the surface of a dresser, a shelf, or a little counter space. It doesn't have to be big or fancy, but it should be neat and tidy. Some basic elements of an ancestor altar include the following:

- Small table or other workable surface
- A tablecloth/altar cloth
- An offering dish
- An offering cup
- Candle and candleholder

- Incense and incense holder

- Images of beloved dead/other ancestor forms

You don't need all of these, but they are helpful elements. If you want to add more, some people like to add meaningful heirlooms to the altar, like those that belonged to whomever you are revering, or just objects that they would like. You can also add crystals, bones, or other natural materials that strengthen the connection to the spirit world. Some people also make offerings of plants by keeping fresh-cut flowers in a vase on the altar, or they might keep dried herbs, flowers, or plants that preserve well. If you like to grow things, a living plant on the altar can reflect your relationship with the ancestors, and as you tend to it, you tend to your beloved dead. Obviously take good care of the plant and don't neglect it, but don't worry if the plant doesn't make it and dies. Just return it to the earth.

Ancestor altars tend to have similar basic components, but you can tailor them to your preference too. Our relationships with those who have passed are unique and personal, even if they passed long before you were born.

Ancestor Offerings

Making physical offerings to the ancestors is a way to keep the connection strong and the road open for guidance and communication. Some of the more common offerings are food and beverage, but there are other types of exchanges too. A lot of Roma believe that if you are constantly spilling your food and drink while cooking or eating, your ancestors are not getting enough offerings, and you have to step up your game. Working with ancestors is like any other relationship—there is give and take. They might have certain wishes for you, and they are often for your own well-being, or for their healing, or for the healing of your line if that's applicable. They might express these messages to you through the divination tools you use to communicate with them, or however you receive messages with any of the clairsenses. You have free will and can say yes or no to their requests, and you might choose to start or stop working with different ancestors at different times.

Sometimes the things that ancestors ask for might seem trivial and nonsensical but will make sense later. For instance, they might want you to buy yourself a toy and you don't know why, but it triggers some inner-child healing. Or they might want you to learn carpentry, and it just ends up being a very helpful skill. We have some guidelines you can use for making offerings, but offerings are a personal, devotional ritual that you are encouraged to make your own.

Many Roma drink coffee with their ancestors as a morning ritual. Alice Johnson and Katelan Foisy both shared their morning ancestor coffee rituals with us on *Romanistan* podcast (we recommend listening to their episodes). Alice will bring a cup of coffee outside in her garden as an offering to her grandmother, whereas Katelan imagines having coffee with her ancestors and guides, and whispers good intentions into her coffee to bless the day ahead.

How to make an offering:

- Set a plate with a small meal plus a beverage at your dinner table for the ancestors.

- Leave food, like candy, fruit, or whatever else they would like, in the offering dish on your altar.

- Leave water, liquor, wine, coffee, or whatever else your ancestors would like in the offering cup on your altar, or outside somewhere connected to your home, or somewhere meaningful.

- Depending on tradition, you can offer the meal/food offerings to passersby after the living are finished eating, or you can eat it yourself later. You can also compost the food if that's appropriate.

- Some people will leave these things where their ancestors are buried or otherwise laid to rest.

- You can also leave offerings where there is running water (ocean, lakes, river, etc.), in caves, bogs, or other places in nature that feel appropriate.

Non-food offerings:

- Money (especially coins)
- Incense
- Tobacco/cigars
- Fresh flowers
- Lottery tickets
- Jewelry
- Trinkets
- Playing cards
- And more ... you'd be surprised what they request

Animism and You

Many Roma are animistic, meaning we believe that everything has a spirit. This can look different from vitsa to vitsa, family to family, but in essence it looks like treating the environment around you, animals, people, plants, objects, earth, wind, stars, and moon with reverence and respect. The Earth is our ancestor too, as is the Universe.

Connecting with Plants

Flowers, trees, vegetables, herbs, plants of all kinds all have their own spirit. You can communicate with plants the same way you do with ancestors and guides through meditation or divination tools of your choice. Jezmina's mom kept a beautiful garden and used to grow as much of their food as possible, and she used to take a notebook out there with her and write down the messages she got from her plants. She said her flowers spoke in poetry. Some people consider plants to be ancestors as well, especially culturally significant plants. Think about the plants that you feel most connected with and try out your favorite divination tools to develop a deeper relationship with them. Ask them questions with a pendulum, get their advice through tarot, or brew a tea of your favorite herbs and see what they have to say in a tea-leaf reading.

Altar Plants and Flowers

If you like keeping plants alive, living plants are a wonderful addition to your altar. If this is too much pressure, or if you think you'll take it too hard if they die, then dried flowers or herbs, or fresh-cut flowers are nice options too. You can work with the plant spirit or essence in your dreams and ask for them to assist you.

Living Plants for Home and Bedroom

Plants have their own associations and meanings, so you can research your favorites and see what kind of energy they're bringing into the home. For instance, poisonous plants like datura, belladonna, henbane, etc. are great to grow near your bed for altered states or dreaming, but do not ingest, and don't grow them if you have pets who munch on plants. Plants don't need to be psychoactive to have a magical effect, however. They all have their gifts.

Some of our other favorite indoor plants:

- Aloe
- Cactus of Any Variety
- Catnip
- Holy Basil (Tulsi)
- Peace Lily
- Philodendron
- Pitcher Plant
- Pothos
- Rosemary
- Snake Plant
- Spider Plant
- Venus Fly Trap

Research how to care for the plants you're drawn to so your plants can really thrive. Make sure that none of them are toxic to your pets. Develop a relationship with your plants. Talk to them and listen to what they say. Write down their messages. Invite them into your dreams, and if possible, keep them near where you sleep, perhaps hanging in the windows by your bed, or perched on your nightstand.

Dried Herbs and Flowers

If keeping plants alive stresses you out, dried bundles of herbs hung from the ceiling or window or arranged in a vase near where you sleep are just as great. Connect with them the same way you would a living plant. Give them love, and ask them for guidance.

Some suggestions for dried flowers and herbs for the home:

- Hawthorn berries on the branch

- Hydrangea

- Lavender

- Pussy Willows

- Rosemary

- Roses

- Thyme

Relationships with the Elements

Air, fire, water, and earth. Wind, volcanoes, oceans, and mountains. The elements make us and make our environment. We have all of the elements within us but in different proportions, so to strike a balance internally, you need to connect with the right elements. For instance, both of us tend to be anxious, and we find water soothes us, so we make sure to check in with our local rivers, lakes, and oceans and develop relationships with them since they do us so much good. Developing a relationship with an element is as simple as talking to it. You can thank the water for its blessings, for nurturing you and the land and animals, for calming you, for anything.

You can bring offerings to your favorite elements, whether that's a mountain path or a little creek, and you can give fruits, honey, wine, juice, or other gifts that are good for the land and won't harm any animals who might come upon them. You can ask the elements for support, guidance, or wisdom, but just like any friendship, there's give and take.

CHAPTER 9

The Ethics of Fortune-Telling

Fortune-telling deals with people's lives, secrets, hopes, dreams, beliefs, loves, mistakes, struggles, and ambitions. The potential for messiness is great if you don't have a solid moral compass yourself. Everyone has their own values they live by and experiences and beliefs that inform them, but we're lending you some of our compass points to help you navigate readings for other people, whether you're reading as a friend or as a professional. We tend to write from a more professional perspective because of the tradition of this work as real labor, but it all applies however you're engaging with reading, even if it's just for yourself.

Jezmina's Grandma's Fortune-Telling Ethics

My grandma gave me these rules when I started reading, and I like to share them whenever I teach any divination classes. They're a good set of rules to work with.

- **Don't tell people that they are going to die or that their loved ones are going to die.** It's never helpful. You're not an all-powerful deity, and you don't know for certain. In the case of someone reading about a loved one who's ill and dying, and wants to know how it's going to play out, it's okay to guide them through, but still avoid making predictions about when the person will die. Focus instead on helping the person process their grief.

- **If there is bad news, give any warnings as good advice.** Don't scare people. If there's no way to do this, don't say anything. For instance, if someone asks what it's going to be like at a new job and a lot of difficult tarot cards come up, don't say, "It's going to be a nightmare and your new boss is a monster." Focus on giving good advice on adjusting to new responsibilities and personalities, and remind them that they can use the job as a stepping stone to a better one if they still don't feel like it's a good fit. Be honest, but in a way that's actually helpful and heartening.

- **You don't know everything. Let people talk for themselves.** It's okay for you to check in and ask if they can relate to what comes up in the reading, how they feel about certain advice, and if there's anything they want to ask or share. It makes people feel cared for and gives them space to process, and it helps you be a better reader with more context.

- **Don't tell people what to do with their lives.** Help them figure out what they need and how to move forward. Most of us want to know what to do, but don't want to be told what to do. You can make it clear that this is what the reading suggests, but things change and your client has free will. They can do what they want. However, sometimes people will come to you and say, "Just tell me what to do!" Even in that case, give them advice, but remind them that they are in control of their own path.

- **Trust your instincts and intuition, and be open to learning.** Intuition is not necessarily rational and can come to you through any of your senses at any time, especially if you're practicing your intuition exercises. You might have a strong but random thought/image/word/scent/taste/emotion pop up as you're reading for someone, and it's okay to say, "Okay, I don't know what this is about, but I'm getting this message. Does this mean anything to you?" Most of the time, it does, and even if it doesn't, it probably will later. The more you do this, even if you feel a little silly or like you could be mistaken, the more you learn about how your intuition works, and about your client.

- **Never lie.** This is straightforward. Don't mislead or otherwise lie to people. Don't just gas them up, or misrepresent a situation for your own gain or anyone else's.

- **It's not about you. Take your ego out of it.** Fortune-telling is not an opportunity to flex your psychic muscles and show everyone how powerful you are. You don't have to prove anything to anyone, and don't take it personally if you're not everyone's favorite reader. It is a service, and it is meant to help those who come to you. Be humble, and use your talents for good.

Fortune-Telling Is Not Therapy

While fortune-telling can be therapeutic, it is not a replacement for therapy. If someone is struggling with mental illness, trauma, addiction, or another issue that feels beyond your ability, it is good practice to suggest help or community support in a nonjudgmental way. It's a good idea to have numbers for local shelters and suicide crisis hotlines on hand if you're reading for the public.

Sometimes people are afraid to seek the help they need and just want someone to tell them it's going to be alright, but if fortune-tellers are meant to help people sort through their problems, then one of the ways we should do that is by directing them to the right professionals or specialists if they need one. You don't need to force them, but you can help destigmatize mental health support, addiction counseling, and other support that everyone deserves access to, should they want it. Both of us have survived trauma, and we have mental illnesses, neurodivergence, and physical illnesses. We go to therapists, doctors, and take our medicine. Fortune-telling and spirituality are great, but they are not cure-alls.

Privacy and Confidentiality

Your clients need to be able to depend on your discretion. You can't be gossiping about them. Every community feels like a small community once you become familiar enough with everyone. You need to be a safe place for people to talk about all kinds of drama; you can't be the drama. Your job is to help the person navigate sticky situations as an impartial viewer, not get involved in them yourself.

No Judgment

You're not here to judge anyone, nor should you make anyone feel judged. If people are trying to work through something, or to heal, they need a space where they can be totally honest and feel safe and accepted. Let's use sobriety as an example. If a client relapses with drugs or drinking, you can use divinatory tools to talk to them about getting back on track, but only if they're open to it, and there's no need to shame them or act like you know better. At the same time, you are not a rehab clinic or a specialist. Usually the reading will bring up themes of health, structure, community support, and the like that make it clear it's time to get into therapy, call their sponsor, head to a meeting, or go to rehab. You can offer these as options and brainstorm with your client to see what kind of care they think is best, or encourage them to reach out to someone who can help them make that choice. Give them the space to accept that they need help and feel okay asking for it. Sobriety is a tough journey. Be compassionate and encouraging.

Infidelity is a popular topic at the reading table. Oftentimes people come in when they are torn between lovers, or have been waiting for their lover to leave their spouse and they're starting to doubt it will ever happen, or they feel guilty because they cheated and regret it and now they don't know what to do. Sometimes they feel like they can't tell anyone but you, so your discretion, understanding, and compassion are very important. Even if it's a situation you can't relate to or you think you could never find yourself in, that's not your place to say. You might be helping them, but it's still none of your business. Your client needs the clarity to understand the situation and themselves better, and make good decisions from there. It's important to pay attention to what the divinatory tools say, not your personal opinion on marriage, dating, separation, divorce, loyalty, monogamy, polyamory, cheating, or anything else. Most of the time, probably 80% in our experience, the people cheating are actually not trying to hurt anyone else. They're feeling torn, brokenhearted, confused, neglected, lonely, desperate, or any number of painful emotions, and they're just trying to find love and happiness. That's something you can empathize with. Occasionally you get a real piece of work who is selfish and likes causing chaos, but those people are not willing to do the spiritual and emotional work of healing, and usually don't stick around as clients when they realize that's what you're about. So just help people from where they are. Don't try to turn them into your idea of moral perfection.

One area that we are very firm about is if someone discloses that they are in an abusive relationship or situation, we pause the reading for the moment and get more information. Are they afraid for their life? Do they have kids, and are the kids safe? Do they have anywhere to go? What's their support system like? This is where those shelter and hotline numbers come in handy. You can't save anyone, but you can encourage them to get appropriate help and get out of that abusive situation as soon as possible, because no one deserves abuse. Continuing the reading from this point is okay and can help them gain clarity on how to proceed, but we always encourage people to leave abusive situations as soon and as safely as possible, and try to provide them with resources, and encourage them to ask their support system for help.

It's so important not to be judgmental in situations like this as well because victims are so manipulated and shamed that it keeps them stuck where they are, and the United States, where we are writing this book, does not have great systems for people fleeing abuse, so they might not have any of the resources they need to leave, and they could face some terrible treatment as they're seeking help. And sometimes there are kids and pets involved, and financial difficulties, and a fear of violent retaliation, so leaving is not always as straightforward as we would like it to be. It's your job to be loving, understanding, and accepting, and to urge them to get support where they can, and go toward safety. You can always light a candle for them or pray on their behalf (free of charge, of course) if you're feeling like you wish you could do more but there's nothing left to do.

When You Really Need to Talk about a Client

The only time you are ethically required to break confidentiality and the no-judgment rule is when you know a child, elder, or dependent is currently being abused, or if your client discloses that they plan to harm or kill someone. It's very rare, but it's happened to us, and we made the reports to the relevant authorities, and the authorities handled it from there. There are different laws in different states about this, so if this situation arises, do your research and seek counsel. Better to make a report that could save someone than to ignore it and regret it.

Manipulation

It's hard to describe, but you know it when you see it. This should go without saying, but it's unethical to convince people that you have the answers to all their problems, and at a steep price. If someone messages you online and says you have a curse on you, and for $500 they can lift it, and only they can lift it, they are scamming you. If they say they can sell you an expensive candle that will make your lover leave their spouse, they are scamming you. If they say you need to buy a special crystal to heal your broken soul or let a loved one move on to the afterlife, they are scamming you. And so on.

Don't be susceptible to this, and don't do anything that looks like this to anyone else. With that said, we practice candle and crystal magic, but the distinction is the threat. A good fortune-teller will not make you feel like you're in danger if you don't buy something or work with them. Readers are allowed to charge what they want, but you should never feel like you are in imminent danger, or that something bad will happen to you or someone else if you don't buy from them.

Power Dynamics

There is a power dynamic between you and your client that you need to be aware of. That's why you should not have romantic or sexual relationships with your clients. If they start out a client, keep it that way. Keep it professional. If you want to date and have a romantic interlude with a client, you need to have an open and honest conversation about it. They might be building you up as some kind of spiritual savior who will fix their life, and that would not be a relationship of equals. If something boundary-crossing does happen, or if you decide to change your relationship with a client from professional to personal, then they should not be your client anymore after that. There's no going back. Paulina has done this, and it did not work out. Please take our advice on this one.

It's okay to give your romantic partner or friends a reading, like you would give them advice on anything on their mind, but have healthy boundaries with them too. Jezmina's go-to move used to be a palm reading on a first date. It's a great way to size up the character of a potential partner, a good excuse to hold hands and make eyes in the candlelight, and a cute way to get to know someone better relatively quickly. Just be aware of how you present yourself, and don't make it seem like you're the all-powerful guru with all the answers. That's weird, and not true. Keep it light, and use it as an opportunity to share interests and connect.

Consent

Seek consent as much as possible with everything you do. It's good to make sure you're on the same page as your clients. If you're working with someone new, make sure that you explain your reading style and what to expect, and give them some choices for the kind of reading that they want. You might start by asking if they've had a reading before. If it's their first reading and they're nervous, they usually voice their qualms here, and you have an opportunity to comfort them.

We like to give a preamble that palmistry is great for looking into your personality traits and nature, and how that affects the broad strokes of your past, present, and future. Tarot and tea-leaf or coffee reading is helpful if you're more interested in now and the near future, or if you have any specific questions, or if you just want to see what message is coming up for you. We let the client pick which tools are best suited for them based on what they're looking for. You can check and see if they have any questions or intentions they want to look into, or any context they want to give, or if they just want to leave it open to whatever comes up. That way they can already start customizing the reading and know what to expect. If your reading style includes touch of any kind, always ask permission, and tell them what to expect before you do it, and let them know they can stop or change their position anytime you want.

Reading about Others and Consent

This is another time when it becomes clear that you are reading a Romani book on fortune-telling. We understand why some readers feel it's unethical for them to read about what a client's ex or someone else is doing or thinking without getting that ex's consent. We would be out of business if we had rules like that, and honestly, it just doesn't seem that bad to us. It's not any different than asking a mutual friend what that person is up to, if they're thinking about you, etc. If you're ethically okay with that, we're okay with it too.

Survival fortune-telling walks a more realistic line between right and wrong, which are sometimes relative concepts anyway. It's fine if you disagree with us about this. Personally, however, we will tell you how your ex is doing, but we're going to try to do it in a way that helps you reframe the situation in a healthier perspective and move on if necessary.

Dependence

Sometimes clients start to depend on you in ways that are not healthy or financially sustainable for them. Even if someone has all the money in the world, if they think they need to consult you for every little decision, there is something wrong there, and it is your responsibility to create and maintain healthy boundaries before it gets to that point. Ideally, you should be empowering your clients to develop and trust their own intuition and sense of self.

Sometimes you might need to say that you have only a certain amount of availability to see them, if they're relying on you too much. Use your readings to help them build confidence in themselves, and suggest other resources for support, like therapy, if they don't have them already.

Your Own Boundaries

You don't have to read for someone if you don't want to. You don't have to put up with rudeness, creepiness, or anything else that feels off. You can refund people and ask them to leave if they are being inappropriate or making you feel unsafe or, depending on how much time and effort you've put into the reading already, just ask them to leave. You can screen your clients, and you can listen to your intuition. Not everyone needs or deserves to have access to you. You have to look out for yourself because no one else is going to, so maintain good boundaries and say no whenever you need to.

Don't Get Too Personal

You can relate to a client without explaining why. You might have a client going through a divorce, and if you are also divorced, that might help you give better advice, but there is no need to actually tell your client about what went down in your own relationship. Their reading is not your time to share. Sometimes clients might ask you specific questions about yourself and it's okay to answer, but you don't need to reveal more than is comfortable, or talk so much that it bites into their time. Jezmina sometimes walks with a cane, for instance, and clients occasionally ask what happened. It's fine to say it's a chronic illness, or nerve pain, or whatever, and move on, but there's no need to go into your medical history. Talk to your friends and family about yourself for sure, and any professionals you work with, but not a client.

Fortune-Telling and Privilege

Roma's relationship with fortune-telling is shaped by persecution, and many of the anti-fortune-telling laws in the US came into existence to target Roma and BIPOC (Black, Indigenous, People of Color) who have also worked spiritual or divination jobs as survival trades. If you are a non-Romani person (gadje) and particularly if you are white, or white passing, there is a privilege you have in this industry (and elsewhere) that non-white people do not have. Both of us have experienced racism, and so have many of our friends and family who appear visibly Romani, or even just ethnically ambiguous. If your skin is dark, you're more likely to experience racism anywhere you go, and fortune-telling is included in that. In the US, there are some police departments that have dedicated "Gypsy task forces" that look out for "Gypsy scams." This is well documented and easy to research. Many of these task forces are just exercises in racial profiling and operate under gross misinformation as well.

We're not saying it's easy to be a white person, or that white people don't suffer sexism, ableism, poverty, trauma, or anything else hard. They do, and life is hard for everyone everywhere. We're just saying that skin color or any other racialized feature opens up a different set of problems to face. It's important to be aware of that and use your relative privilege in this area to lift up others, especially if you are using their ancestral practices to make a living. Pay it back to the communities you learn from directly or indirectly and be a good ally. Be aware of the way that you present yourself, of cultural appropriation, of the language and images you use to promote yourself, and uplift Roma and other BIPOC creators with your platform or other resources.

Educate Yourself

There is trauma-informed training out there, and training on working with BIPOC populations and LGBTQIA+ folks with awareness and sensitivity. We highly recommend you read books, listen to podcasts, watch documentaries, do courses, and educate yourself on other people's histories, struggles, and lived experiences. You don't want to be ignorant or accidentally harmful to someone because you don't know better and didn't bother researching. Everyone has a backstory, and many people are navigating systems of oppression in ways that you may or may not understand. You don't have to be a social worker, doctor, activist, scholar, and therapist all in one to be a good reader, but if you're dealing with people's lives, you should understand how complicated it can be to be a person. The information is available!

Jezmina on Education

I'm a trauma-informed yoga teacher, and the required training was incredibly helpful for yoga students navigating trauma as well as fortune-telling clients. I also worked as both an adjunct English and writing professor, and as a middle school teacher specializing in English, writing, social studies, and art. In order to meet the kids' needs and learn the subject matter backwards and forwards, I had to make sure I was informed too, so I dove into Indigenous history, Black history, and the histories of other marginalized ethnic groups, the history of colonization and subsequent decolonization movements, feminist history, LGBTQIA+ history, child labor rights, disability rights, and so on.

This time as a teacher was so valuable because teaching requires that you are always learning. You can't be the most informed person on every topic at all times, and you can't be perfect, but you can be open to learning and willing to revise and reflect on your perspective.

Paulina on Education

When I was seventeen, I had just gotten married according to custom, and I was expected to make a living through fortune-telling at my in-laws' shop. There were many readers in the area, especially since this is an up-and-coming profession, and I sought after a way to stand out. Originally, I expressed wanting to take some psychology courses (*Psychology for Dummies* was a book I read as a young teen) because I found so many parallels in reading people spiritually and reading people psychologically, but I received negative feedback from family when I mentioned it. Schooling was too "Americanized" for us.

Eventually, when I opened my own shop, I decided to get certified in life coaching. It was not difficult, and I found it to be a great tool alongside holistic healing. I created a spiritual wellness program, and life coaching is a big part of it to this day. I did end up taking a few psychology courses, and I'm currently pursuing my higher education, but in the past, I made the best with what I had. Life coaching allowed me to stand out as a reader online and in my business altogether.

No Spiritual Bypassing

Spiritual bypassing is a term coined by author and psychotherapist John Welwood that describes how people can use spirituality to dismiss difficult emotions and reasonable reactions to trauma, poverty and classism, displacement, oppression, discrimination, illness, etc. Sometimes certain emotions like sadness, rage, grief, and vengeance are labeled as "low vibrational," and interestingly, these are the kinds of feelings that fuel resistance to injustice, and revolutions. There is the misguided belief that some emotions are better or "higher vibe" than others, like love, joy, and peace, and that these are the only acceptable emotions. However, being at peace with an abusive system is beneficial only to the abusers. It becomes clear right away that the people who spiritually bypass others have something to gain, either maintaining a power structure that's in their favor, or simply excusing themselves from engaging with real human struggle. Often spiritual systems from other cultures are misunderstood and misappropriated by spiritual bypassers to justify their beliefs and actions.

CHAPTER 10

How to Be Convincing

The ability to be convincing transcends instruments like crystal balls and tarot cards—it's an art, a delicate balance of perception, communication, and presence. There are subtle yet impactful ways to authentically weave your divination without resorting to gimmicks or manipulation. You can be a talented, accurate reader and still be unconvincing if you don't have the right demeanor. Because so many Roma work this job as a survival trade, over the centuries we have perfected our presentation. Whether you are planning on reading professionally or just for friends, these tips will help you deliver more powerful and resonant readings. Outside of readings, though, being convincing is a skill that will serve you everywhere.

Paulina on Being Convincing

Growing up, my family and I depended on fortune-telling to make a living and survive. In my closed community, it was one of the only professions women were allowed to work, and the only profession available to me. This was made clear to me early on in my childhood. Like many Romani kids in traditional communities, I was taken out of school in middle school because my family was preparing me to become a wife, mother, and fortune-teller. I cover this in more detail in our podcast *Romanistan*, and the *Los Angeles Times* podcast *Foretold* about leaving my community and arranged teen marriage.

So, you can guess that stakes were high, and the game was on. It's not that we needed to convince people we could see the future, but we needed to convince them we were masters in our craft and that they could depend on us for a raw, culturally rooted, and truthful experience. With that said, yes, predictions come true, and I believe in the intuition that my ancestors and I possess. This book isn't about just any fortune-telling, it's about Romani or, as I call it, Gypsy fortune-telling. We could not afford to make mistakes or make people feel uncomfortable. We never made clients feel like we were more or less than them. We just invited them in as equals, with an open mind and heart. That's what was convincing. All the women in my family told me, "You will never be a true success if you don't believe in what you are saying, whether it's good or bad. You have to convince yourself first and most importantly. You have to believe in yourself and your craft." The elders would say, "If you are not completely sure about something, you should say that. Express that you have a slight feeling of possibility about a prediction or statement, as opposed to telling the client you are certain when you are not." Honesty gains trust, and I cannot emphasize that enough.

When I was twelve years old, I had already left school, and my mother told me I was ready to do my first professional reading. I grew up poor in my childhood years, and, like I said earlier, our business was our livelihood. Before I met with my client, my mother told me that I better be convincing or we wouldn't eat that day. So, although you may not be able to put that immense pressure on yourself, you can indeed challenge yourself. For example, buy a new piece of clothing only if you successfully gave a reading that week. Of course, I wouldn't want you to stress, but I know working under pressure worked for me. It sounds a little unhealthy, because it probably is, but you are not reading any old divination book. You're reading a Romani one. Romani people have experienced an extraordinary amount of cumulative trauma throughout the centuries, and it's passed from our ancestors to us through stories, actions, and feelings. Now, it comes up in our daily lives, our work, our books, and our hearts, so I believe it's important to note.

My first reading went well, though. I walked into our small office room and sat down with the new customer. My mother lingered behind me to cut in just in case I was doing a bad job. The worst part was the first five seconds. I laid out the first set of cards face down, of course, because I was a kid and nervous as hell. My mom interrupted me and reminded me to flip the cards over so I could actually read them. The client chuckled a little with us and, after I finished, said that she enjoyed the reading. My mother and I still laugh about it today.

Overall, you have to believe in yourself and meet yourself where you're at. You will make mistakes, but don't let the mistakes ruin the outcome. Shake it off.

Jezmina on Being Convincing

I had to be convincing from a young age, but for different reasons than Paulina. Some of my first clients were horses, and horses always know if you're nervous, and if you're nervous, then they're nervous. And the last thing you want to do is make a horse nervous. Let me explain.

When my grandmother came to the US, she was already familiar with working with animals because of her stepfather, the farmer who protected her and her mother and siblings. Years later, when my grandmother and her husband moved to New Hampshire into a condemned house with barely any heat but a good amount of land, she wanted to rescue a couple of horses, even though they were extremely poor. She wanted to teach her children to ride, and she wanted them to teach the neighborhood kids to ride, and make a little money using her old-world skills. They made it work because they had no choice—my mom, auntie, and uncles started working as kids to put food on the table, and my mother and auntie continued working with horses into their adulthood. I grew up around horses, but never was a rider because my mother felt that I chose fortune-telling, so she refused to teach me to ride or even handle horses because I "chose my path."

My first jobs in rural New Hampshire, starting when I was a preteen and into my teen years, were fortune-teller, dishwasher at a seedy restaurant, and eventually, horse charmer. In the late 90s and early 2000s in New Hampshire, people were shy of anything that looked like witchcraft, so fortune-telling wasn't in big demand. My mom and auntie could get me some gigs telling fortunes at their friends' parties, but not often enough for me to master my work. If I was going to be successful, I needed more work with higher stakes. That's where the horses came in. People at the barns where my mom and aunt worked who would balk at getting their own fortunes read were desperate to know why their prized horse was lame three weeks before a show for seemingly no reason. They would try anything, even a fortune-teller kid.

"If you're a really good reader, you should be able to read a horse. That's the real test," my mother told me after she had arranged a few horse clients. Horses are harder to read because you don't share a common language. I would have to go off of pure energy. This would be great practice, and I was grateful, but I was a little afraid of horses. I didn't know how to handle them. Some of the horses were aggressive, unpredictable, and even violent. Especially my first client, whom I'll call Bitey McKickerson. He was a thousand-pound horse, and I was just a thirteen-year-old kid who would be enclosed in his stall, trying find out why he was terrorizing the barn hands.

"You can't be nervous," my mother said. "If you're nervous, the horses won't trust you, and they'll panic, or worse." I couldn't help but feel my mother was taking delight in this challenge. I had to have grit like her to pull it off. It wasn't all tea-leaf reading and good vibes with Grandma anymore. I had to have nerves of steel now.

My first client, Bitey McKickerson, was grouchy in the mornings. He always bit the barn hands, kicked at any target, and was generally a nightmare when being led out into the paddock. My mother was not going to supervise me, because this was the test. So before walking into that stall and closing the door behind me, trapping myself in a dark box with a huge animal who loved to chomp, I spent almost fifteen minutes doing the cloud meditation my grandmother taught me (you can find this meditation in Chapter 2) outside of his stall, clearing my mind and opening it to god, Sara la Kali, my spirit guides, my ancestors, and even Bitey himself. I asked for protection, and I asked to do a good job, because this horse was clearly unhappy about something, and I wanted to help him and everyone who worked with him.

I looked at Bitey and said, "I'm going to come into your stall now if that's okay. I'm here to help you." He seemed alright with that, or at least indifferent, so I went in. When I stepped into that stall, I kept my breaths slow and deep, despite the smell of urine and manure that I never really got used to. The breath was my protective thread that would keep me calm, focused, and connected. I had to convince that horse that I knew what I was doing and that I belonged there so he wouldn't freak out and take a bite out of my face.

I said, "I'm going to put my hands on you if that's okay," but I didn't just say it. I imagined sending it to him telepathically too. My grandmother had taught me hands-on healing, so I placed my palms on him and asked if I could connect with him. Almost immediately, I heard a rushed voice inside my head say, "They play the radio so loud and I don't like the music, and it hangs right in my stall, and it drives me crazy all night, and I just get so tired and angry because I can't get any peace, it's way too loud, and the barn hands are singing along in the morning and I just **can't take it**." There was country music playing at all times in the barn, but I never thought about where it came from. I looked up and I saw that, yes, there was a small radio hanging at the top of his stall door. Small but loud. The way that the horse "talked" to me wasn't in English really—it was like my brain was translating his thoughts and emotions into my language. He was telling me he had heard better music before, and I understood that he meant classical. He didn't like country music at all.

I thanked him, petted him, and told him I would relay his message to everyone. I gave him some apples, carrots, and a peppermint, and he seemed much happier. When I told the barn hands and his owner what he said, they thought it was odd, but they did move the radio to the other side of the barn, lowered the volume, and said they wouldn't sing when they were near his stall. They even reluctantly promised to play classical music at night instead of their favorite country station. And Bitey McKickerson showed his gratitude by being a sweet angel in the morning from that point on. No biting, no kicking, no terrorizing.

After word of Bitey's transformation got around the barn, my clients picked up, and horses were telling me all their secrets. One was lame only because her shoes were bothering her. Her owner called the farrier, who redid them, and she was back to her old self in time for her show. One skittish horse confessed he was afraid of tarps, and that's why he was spooking in the arena. And so on and so on. To read for these horses, I had to be perfectly calm and confident, not just because they might get scared if I was scared, but because I had to really believe in my ability in order to get their messages and not think I was crazy. Every time I believed in myself, I saw results, and the horses were happy. I conquered my fear of horses and got some of the best practice I could ask for. My mother was right—if I could read a horse, I could read anyone. I see now that my family was creating high stakes for me to learn quickly.

Confidence

From our stories above, you see how important confidence is if you're going to be convincing. We said confidence, though, not cockiness. Confidence isn't about promising the moon but about skillfully navigating the tools, being a good listener and a clear speaker, and offering authentic interpretations. It's important not to be arrogant or act like you have all the answers. No one has all the answers. Clients are looking for guidance, however, and your confidence is like a compass for them. But be secure enough to remind them that they can take what resonates from your reading and do what they want, and that things change, and they have free will. You're not trying to control them, and you should make peace with the fact that you can't control anyone (nor should you).

If you tend to be nervous or timid, this is a wonderful opportunity to step into a place of power. When you stand firm in your interpretations, it allows clients to trust the process and let the conversation unfold. It might help build your confidence to check in with your client and ask if they can relate to what's coming up, and you can also ask what is resonating with them so far. If you're feeling uncertain as you're going along, hearing what is clicking with your client can make you feel more self-assured and give you the mettle to keep going in your reading. If you are making suggestions to clients about possible changes or approaches, you can pause to ask them if they have a sense of what that would look like more concretely for them. For instance, if you're giving a reading and you're intuiting that they need to network more for their career, you can pause and say, "Do you know whom you would reach out to, or where to start?" and if they have no idea, you know that you need to use your tools to help them. If they already know what they should do, you can validate their good instincts and move on to another point. These are good practices in general for any reading, but especially helpful if you're feeling anxious about your abilities. It makes the reading more of a collaborative effort, and ultimately, more beneficial for the client.

No Apologies (Unless You Really Owe One)

Sometimes clients have unreasonable expectations for your abilities. A situation that we run into a lot is the client who wants to know when and where they're going to meet their true love, despite the fact that they haven't attempted dating or even done anything social in the last five years, and don't plan on it. They don't want to try dating apps, or chance speed dating, or be set up by friends, or join any clubs. And they haven't been to therapy or done any kind of work on themselves emotionally or spiritually to try to understand their trouble connecting with people, and they aren't interested. If someone doesn't like the way they do things, then they can hit the road.

Despite all of this, they essentially want you to tell them which grocery store to walk into so they can bump into the person of their dreams, ready and waiting for them, and construct a real-world meet-cute so they brush hands while reaching for the grapefruit, and then they're living happily ever after. Don't ever apologize for your client's absurdity, but don't make them feel bad about it either. Both will make them lose respect for you, and you will lose credibility in their eyes. Most of the time people just don't know better, and sometimes they are silly. The latter cannot be helped. However, you should point out that no one can tell the future like this, no matter how talented, because whether they're asking when they'll get rich, find love, or finally be happy, it's all about the choices they make, and the work they put in. A reading can help guide them in the right direction toward change, but they have to make the changes if they want to see results. They have to try. No one has a magic formula in this life. It's your job to firmly and kindly bring them back down to earth. Don't let them shake you. Stay confident, and be warm about it.

We've also both met readers who, upon meeting a new client, immediately apologize for not being able to predict the future and say that they hope their new client is not disappointed. Why would you lead with your worst foot forward like that? Don't say what you can't do. Instead, say what you can do. This is a better way to establish boundaries, guidelines, and expectations. Tell them that you can help them see with more clarity what is going on around them and navigate with their best path and outcome in mind. They are responsible for their choices and efforts, just as they were before they walked into this reading. You are giving them your time, attention, intuition, and insight. That is a valuable service. Be humble but be self-assured. They want to feel like they made the right choice coming to you, and they did. No apologies necessary.

The only time you should apologize as a reader is if you genuinely do something worth apologizing for, like if you're running late, or if you forget their name, misgender them, bump into them, spill their tea, or somehow offend them. And with honest mistakes or human error, it's usually better to say thank you first. "Thank you so much for your patience waiting for me," or "Thank you for correcting me on your name/pronouns." This is so much more gracious and graceful than apologizing profusely and making a bigger deal out of a small moment than necessary, which just makes everyone uncomfortable. If you're overly apologetic, you might make them feel like they need to emotionally caretake your fragility, which is not how you want a client to feel. Set the tone, always.

The Psychology of Calm and Balanced

Picture a serene lake reflecting the moonlit night—a tranquil scene that draws you in. Don't you just want to stay there forever? As a reader, maintaining a calm and balanced demeanor is how you draw others into the mystical experience. When you exude tranquility, it changes the energy in the room like an intoxicating perfume. Your client wants to breathe it in. You create a safe space for clients to open up and receive your insights with your behavior, tone, and mannerisms. You give them solace, a haven where they can share their innermost thoughts without fear or reservation. Your calm presence acts as a mirror, reflecting with assurance that there is wisdom in every twist of their journey and that they are capable and empowered.

You don't have to be this calm and balanced person all the time because it's not possible. Life is complicated, messy, and stressful, and we get tired, sick, and burnt out. But you do need to try to be calm and balanced when you're reading for yourself and others. The cleansing and protection practices we discuss in chapter 2 are meant to be done regularly, if not daily. They will help you find this place of peace over and over again. It might be helpful to think of yourself as being in character or stepping into a persona so you can leave behind your everyday life and inhabit a different headspace with a very specific purpose, to practice divination and help others. You can always get back to your personal concerns and daily responsibilities later. They will wait for you.

For this reason, it is also important that you practice good self-care and not read for people when you cannot be calm and balanced. People are coming to you with their lives, and you don't want to do them a disservice because you can't center yourself. Be mindful about when you schedule readings (so don't book a client right after your therapy session or something stressful), be aware of how many readings you can reasonably handle in a day because it is tiring, it's okay to reschedule folks or have sick days if you need to, and make sure to take breaks as needed in between clients so you can take care of yourself.

Our personal stories earlier in this chapter show that high stakes and high pressure can yield great results, and sometimes our circumstances are just that way, whether we like it or not. But you're not meant to run yourself into the ground. You will perform better in the long run if you learn when to challenge yourself and when to rest. Calm and balanced.

Navigating Big Emotions

Sometimes in readings, people will share very sad, traumatic, or difficult experiences with you, and it's very important that you stay calm and balanced then too. Acknowledge how difficult their experiences are without getting swept up in their emotions or your own reactions or opinions. Stay compassionate but centered with phrases like, "That sounds incredibly difficult," or "You've been through so much in just a year." Speak to them in a way that acknowledges both their struggle and their resilience. It's important to be aware of your reactions and what you say, because imagine how awful it would be to go to a reader with your traumatic story, and the reader is the one crying, gasping, expressing shock or disbelief, and acting out about it more than you are.

Your clients need to feel like you are strong and secure enough to hear what they're going through, because you are there to help. You can't get emotional and make them feel like they need to take care of you. Even if you want to cry while listening to their sad story, it's best to avoid it if you can. You can cry later, after they leave. And you should cry if you need to. But this moment is about them and their pain. If you do get teary despite your best efforts, assure them that you are okay, and that you just really empathize, and tell them to please continue sharing. And if your client is having an emotional release, crying or whatnot, make sure you tell them that they are welcome to feel however they feel, and express it however they need to. Crying is good! It's healthy. Always keep tissues in the room for clients so they can let it out, snot and all. If you stay calm and encouraging while they're crying, they will feel safer, and they will be supported to move through the emotional release more comfortably.

Setting the Stage

Mystical guidance is a craft that requires practitioners to perform a certain role or play a part. Even if you take your divination practice extremely seriously, for most people, what we do is entertainment, and so they expect us to entertain. This is also true because many of the anti-fortune-telling laws in the US, originally meant to target Roma and other BIPOC, have forced readers of all backgrounds to make the disclaimer that their services are for entertainment purposes only, so whether you like it or not, depending on where you live, you might need to market yourself that way. Aside from public perception and legality, your environment really is of the utmost importance. It sets the stage for your performance. How, then, can one be convincingly mystical without resorting to clichés? The first step is dressing your environment to fit the part, and to be inviting, comfortable, and transporting. Whether you are selling readings at a nightclub, working in a shop setting, or giving free readings to your friends and family at your barbeque, your space should be inviting.

Both of us like to have a darker space to hold readings, with black or jewel-toned walls and low lighting from beautiful lamps with colored lamp shades or scarves swathed around them. Changing the lighting makes the client feel as though they are stepping into another world. Bright lighting tends to be associated with corporate spaces, and we are an escape from that world, perhaps even its antithesis. We like to decorate like our families did at home, because if we feel at home, then so do our clients. We love

Turkish rugs, poufs to sit on, and tapestries from West Asia/the Middle East. We tend to prefer raw materials for our furnishings and decorations, like wood, metal, cotton, and glass, as opposed to plastic. We try to use Romani-made goods whenever we can. Romani-made goods are a great way to engage in cultural appreciation. They're made for anyone to buy and use. We have a list on our website, *romanistanpodcast.com*.

If we are out and reading at an event, we usually bring a colorful table-cloth for the table, a candle or incense to set the mood and attract people with scent, and maybe a few small crystals that are good for clarity, compassion, and intuition, like amethyst, selenite, fluorite, mangano calcite, or whatever your favorites are. We also bring well-designed business cards with a QR code on the back so people can find us online and even tip us through an app if they don't carry cash. And we make sure the tip jar is stylish, and stuff a $20 bill in there to attract more of the same.

While we tend to decorate Roma-style, that might not feel authentic or appropriate if you aren't Romani, so think about what furnishings and decor speak to you and your own tastes. Keep in mind that no matter your style, you are creating an otherworldly moment and an invitation into a safe and spiritual space. So even if you're just reading for your friends in the afternoon at your apartment, take a moment to light a candle and lay down a pretty tablecloth before you start. Setting the mood makes the experience feel more authentic, unique, and real. Have fun decorating!

Attire and Appearance

Like in any profession, appearance is important. If you are not Romani, you can dress the part of a fortune-teller without dressing up like a Gypsy stereotype. Dressing up as a "Gypsy" perpetuates harmful stereotypes and inaccurately portrays our culture that has faced discrimination and marginalization. Not all Roma are fortune-tellers, but the two of us just so happen to be. Gypsy costumes are often hypersexualized caricatures that reinforce negative and inaccurate perceptions, disregarding the diverse history, traditions, and struggles of Romani people all over the world.

Additionally, it is cultural appropriation, meaning that elements of a marginalized culture are used for fashion or entertainment without understanding or respecting their significance. Present-day Roma and our ancestors before us have faced racism and discrimination merely for wearing our traditional clothing or head coverings in public. When individuals who are not Roma dress up like us in this knockoff facsimile and are celebrated for it, it's a display of privilege and insensitivity because Roma experience harassment and prejudice for looking like Gypsies. Moving forward, we aim to change this with the support of allies and outsiders to foster understanding and respect for our culture.

Dressing appropriately as a divination practitioner or fortune-teller while respecting Romani culture involves thoughtful consideration. Avoiding stereotypical "Gypsy" costumes is crucial (they're trashy polyester embarrassments anyway). Focus on attire that conveys a sense of mystery and wisdom without appropriating or caricaturing Roma. Opt for elegant and enigmatic clothing choices, embracing rich fabrics, layered textures, colors you love, and unique accessories that are empowering to you. Dressing well, not in imitation, but with a nod to the essence of a fortune-teller, is a way to honor the profession without appropriating a marginalized culture. You can also support Romani businesses by purchasing from Romani fashion brands that sell clothing, jewelry, and accessories that are fine for anyone to wear. This is an example of cultural appreciation, not appropriation. Loly by Zita Moldovan, Romani Design, and Classy X Design are just a few Romani brands to get you started. Check our website for more. We recommend you wear what you feel comfortable in, whether it's Romani-made or not, as long as it is respectful and professional.

Our families told us that you need to be clean and neat whenever you start working. So brush your hair, if you have hair, and take a shower, wear deodorant or make sure you smell good, pick out something comfortable and stylish in whatever style you prefer, make sure there are no stains or rips, and wear decent shoes.

The Power of Eye Contact and Posture

We discussed eye contact in chapter 2 for developing your psychic gifts and connecting with the client. It can also be helpful for making you appear to be a more professional and convincing reader, if you and your client are the kind of people who like eye contact and find it comforting. So make eye contact, but do so with sensitivity to the other person's comfort level, and your own.

Do as the elders tell you and sit up straight when reading for someone. It projects a presence that is both grounded and open. This posture signals confidence and authority, enhancing your overall convincing aura.

What If There's Too Much Eye Contact?

If a client is staring at you a little too much and making you feel uncomfortable, Paulina's aunt recommends that you pick up a card, or point to whatever other tool you're using, or gesture to something in the room as an example. It has the dual effect of engaging their attention in what you're doing if you think they are spacing out, but also just breaking the stare so you can regain your bearings and feel more comfortable in your flow.

What If There's Too Little Eye Contact?

We mentioned this earlier, but not everyone likes or can handle eye contact. If a client avoids eye contact, don't press it, and instead focus on the cards, palm, cup, or whatever tool you're using. If you don't like making eye contact, then don't force yourself to be uncomfortable. If you're concerned that the client thinks it might be strange that you're not holding their gaze, and you don't feel like sharing that eye contact isn't your thing, you can say something like, "It's part of my process to stare at the tarot spread as I work," or something to that effect. It sounds professional, and that way you don't need to disclose anything personal to clients if you don't want to.

The Command of a Firm Yet Gentle Voice

In the symphony of your reading, your voice is the melody. Speak with a firm yet gentle tone, loud and clear enough to be heard but soft enough to be soothing. If the client seems to be struggling to hear you, like if they're leaning in or asking you to repeat yourself, or asking questions that seem out of context, they might be hearing impaired, so speak up.

Speak Their Language, Not Down to Them

The language of fortune-telling isn't about grandiose phrases or abstract mystical jargon; it's about connecting with your audience on a human level. Avoid talking down to clients or overexplaining your process. Instead, articulate your insights in a way that resonates with their experiences, using relatable metaphors and explaining any spiritual terms you use quickly and clearly. This bridges the gap between the ethereal and the everyday. By keeping your language accessible, you invite clients to participate with you more fully.

Be Worldly

Be curious about the world around you. When you meet new people socially, ask them about themselves and see what you can learn. It is a quintessentially Romani approach to learn as much as possible from everyone you can. It's what makes you a survivor in a world that is not built for you, and it also makes a good fortune-teller. Go out of your way to learn about other industries, cultures, careers, and experiences. Anyone can walk into your reading room, and intuition can get you part of the way there, but if you actually know something about what it's like to be an abuse survivor, teacher, ex-con, nurse, sex worker, artist, mechanic, teen mom, stockbroker, immigrant, drag queen, engineer, etc., then your intuition is grounded in something real. Learn as much as you can about everything always, and learn from a combination of real-life people and balanced, trusted academic or news sources.

We love that we get to interview Roma from all walks of life on *Romanistan* podcast and learn about their lives, professions, passions, and family histories. Listen to podcasts, watch documentaries, get books from the library, and make use of other free resources where you get to learn about all types of people, subjects, cultures, histories, industries, and more. You don't have to form strong opinions on everything you learn—it just helps to be informed as much as possible. You never know what information or experience will come in handy.

Convincing, Not Manipulative

You don't need to be manipulative to be convincing. You need to be self-aware and self-assured, and to listen to what the client needs. Authenticity is your greatest tool. Strive for a seamless blend of confidence, relatability, and psychological insight. There are always going to be skeptics, but their beliefs are not your problem. Everyone has the right to believe what they believe. Your conviction in your own work is what makes you convincing. At the same time, we do have some advice for dealing with skeptics.

CHAPTER 11

How to Deal with Skeptics

Why so serious? We'll tell you why.

As a new or experienced reader, you probably get a weird little feeling in the pit of your stomach when you think about a skeptic walking into a reading with you and challenging your work. It instantly turns a fun, emotional, and spiritual activity into a very serious matter. You might feel like you need to be defensive and stand up for yourself and your work, but that usually backfires. Being tested is something you may have to get used to if you do this regularly or professionally. Here are some steps you can take to prepare.

Steps for Dealing with Skeptics

Put yourself in the skeptic's shoes. They are paying for services and spending time with you. That's why they are usually serious. They value themselves and are choosing you for a moment in their lives. Understand and accept their skepticism. You don't need to convince them. You only need to perform your service. If you have the mindset of "I'm going to prove you wrong," it's not going to make anything better.

Next, make an effort to create a comfortable atmosphere. Remember, you're about to engage in an energy exchange. Ask if there's anything specific you can do for them, whether it's adjusting the lighting, providing water, or ensuring the room temperature suits them.

It's also a good idea to share a bit about the origins, background, and history of your specialty. Keep it concise and engaging without sounding like a broken record, and keep it short and sweet. Always maintain a calm demeanor when communicating.

Ask them about what brings them to you today. Sometimes skeptics prefer to give you nothing to work from because they are testing you, but check in with them throughout the reading to see if they can connect with what's come up so far.

If they say that they can't relate with the reading, take a moment to back up and see if there's a perspective you're overlooking, and invite them to share their thoughts. If they are just being rude and disagreeable, this genuine effort to clarify and connect with them will usually make them stop. If they really didn't relate to what you said, or understand it, the time you spend finding the thread of the reading with them will probably be appreciated.

It's important not to apologize or get shaken by them if they aren't validating everything you say, or if they are purposefully saying that they can't relate to anything in your reading, no matter how relatable it is. Use this as an opportunity to show how readings can be conversational and collaborative, and are better for it. Let them know that they can ask any questions they want, including questions about your process.

Thank them at the end of the reading for trying you out. They went out on a limb to do something out of their comfort zone. Make them feel appreciated.

By taking these steps, you can foster a more positive and open experience for both you and the skeptic.

What to Do if a Client Argues about Your Prices

Clients need to understand they are paying for your time, energy, and to perform a practice. Because divination is different for everyone, knowing your specialty, and being able to explain what that entails, is crucial, especially with skeptics. Don't apologize for your prices. In fact, do a little research and see how much other readers in your area charge, and make sure you're not undercutting your competition. If a reading is unusually cheap, people won't take it as seriously. If a reading is unusually expensive, people might feel like they're being price gouged, unless you're a reader to the stars or have a lot of experience and a sparkling reputation, in which case, charge your worth.

Both of us choose to offer sliding scale in our personal practice, which means that if people are struggling financially, we can come up with a price that feels reasonable to them based on their income. We encourage people to use this option only if they really need it, and that way we can charge what we need to survive and still be accessible for folks who want to work with us but might not have the means. Because this is our livelihood, we do limit the number of sliding scale clients that we can see a month. But it usually balances out because wealthier clients might tip us well because they have the means.

At the time of writing this, in addition to their private practice, which offers sliding scale, Jezmina works at a shop that has set prices, and it feels important to honor that. If you are unapologetic about your prices, it reminds people that this is a real job and a real service with value. That makes skeptics believe in you a little more and keeps food on your table.

Are You a Skeptic?

We're all skeptical about something. You don't have to get into your deep personal beliefs or your opinions on conspiracy theories to relate to the skeptics who come to you for a reading, but it can help to relate when it's relevant, especially if they're telling you to your face that they're skeptics. They might need reassuring, but not in the way you might think. Bragging about your abilities, talking down to them from your spiritual high horse, or dismissing them is not going to work. Instead, acknowledge your own skepticism in a way that validates them and invites them to try something new in a way that feels comfortable to them.

Paulina's Skepticism

I like to tell skeptical clients that I'm a skeptic too. When discussing my belief in divination, I often draw parallels to my religious upbringing in Catholicism, and how my perspective has over time now shifted from being religious to being spiritual. Somedays, the notion of a higher power and all texts in the Bible resonated deeply, while on other days, I couldn't even wrap my head around it. I realized that I was struggling with Catholicism as a doctrine, and that made me doubt my faith in everything. Despite my many efforts to renounce my belief in God, though, I just couldn't shake the feeling there was something bigger than me, and us, as humans, out there. That's when I realized that I could just believe in what felt true to me and remain skeptical about everything else.

I'm not a Catholic anymore, but I do believe in a higher power, but in a way that's personal to me. Finding a balance became my answer, steering clear of doctrinal extremes. My relationship with my God has never been better. Similar to the fluctuations I experienced in my religious convictions, my outlook on fortune-telling has had an ebb and flow over the years. I've found harmony in my healthy skepticism, and it's become part of my approach to fortune-telling. It makes me a more grounded reader if I take everything with a grain of salt and acknowledge my human fallibility.

Telling my skeptical clients that I know and agree that divination isn't a perfect science helps them trust me more. I'm not going to pretend that I know everything, but I do believe in what I do, and believing in divination and how it can work is personal, like my belief in God. I encourage them to enjoy the ride, and that usually softens their reservations. Transparency is key, and this is a lesson I've gleaned from lived experience. I tell my clients that what unfolds during a fortune-telling session isn't set in stone. My guiding influences in the divinatory arts impressed upon me that fortune-telling is an exploration of the highest probability. It allows for flexibility, and for the client to alter their path by changing their perspective and making decisions. My ancestors literally believed it was invented to be used as a tool to warn against or change the future. In essence, fortune-telling at its best encourages adaptability and a nuanced understanding of the intricate web of life.

In a fortune-telling business, it's reasonable to wonder whether admitting doubts about your own craft or spiritual path could make you seem less credible. But the skeptic is not having doubts about something tried, trusted, and tested, like the work of a shoe cobbler or a pilot. Fortune-telling isn't a science, and it isn't brain surgery, so they don't need to treat it so seriously. When you're open about your struggles or doubts, it builds trust with people. They see you as genuine, not just someone trying to look perfect. It makes the whole experience more authentic and connects you with clients on a deeper level. It brings the human element back into it. So, in the world of fortune-telling, being honest about your own journey can be a key to building strong, meaningful relationships with those seeking guidance. Remember, just because you are being honest, you still need to remain confident, calm, and professional.

Jezmina's Skepticism

I often feel skeptical of other people. If a client comes in saying they're skeptical, I say that it's good to be skeptical, because I know some readers can be unethical and run scams on their clients, or try to manipulate them into being dependent on them, or just tell them what they want to hear. It's tough out there, and people can be sketchy, whether they're telling your fortune or buying you a drink. It makes sense to be cautious. And sometimes people are just not very good with their tools, with no ill intention, and can still do damage. Some readers out there maybe aren't ready to be reading professionally.

Sometimes folks come to me with bad experiences behind them. Maybe readers were cruel and tried to scare them, or were dismissive of their feelings, or tried to bully them into expensive cures that would lift the "curse" they have on them that will supposedly ruin their life if left unchecked. So I get it. I'm very careful about whom I get readings from, too. I very rarely try out a new fortune-teller, to be honest, unless they come highly recommended by someone I trust. If I don't want to read for myself, I usually go to my beloved fortune-teller friends for readings. So I remind my clients that they are the experts on themselves, and they are welcome to take or leave anything I say, correct me if they want to, ask questions, interject information, or sit there quietly. Whatever works for them. There is a power dynamic between reader and client, and I want to keep things feeling as open, comfortable, and boundaried as possible. I check in with them throughout the reading to see how what I'm saying is feeling to them, because letting a stranger peer into your life can feel vulnerable, and I genuinely want them to feel comfortable, understood, and respected.

How to Explain Fortune-Telling

It helps to give some context to the art of divination if folks are feeling uncertain, combative, or maybe a little vulnerable. We find that the following talking points help us with these types of clients.

Tell the History

Fortune-telling garners more respect when it's made clear to your client that it is an enduring tradition that is deeply ingrained in diverse belief systems, interwoven with societal customs and inherited wisdom. The benefits of fortune-telling transcend mere prediction. A reading can touch on historical, familial, and communal narratives, and help you find the red thread to make sense of it all. People may be more willing to regard fortune-telling with appreciation if they understand where it comes from and what its intentions are. We shared the Romani roots of these practices as both a survival tool and a survival trade throughout this book, especially Chapter 1, and you can share what you've learned with them, as well as your own history with your divinatory tools of choice.

You're Human

Fortune-telling is a unique craft because it's all about understanding the spiritual and emotional side of things, the abstract, the relational, and aspirational. A reading can be very practical and grounded, or dive deep into spirit guides and universal mysteries. Either way, it's a more magical approach to life, and it's a very personal and intimate practice. So, being truthful about not having all the answers, and having your own struggles and uncertainties, can actually be a strength. It's like saying, "Hey, I'm human too, and I understand that life is complex and unpredictable." It's never a good idea to get into your own personal struggles in depth because that makes the reading about you, not them, and they have paid for your time and attention. It is helpful, however, to commiserate for a moment about how natural and relatable it is to struggle with perfectionism, self-compassion, or self-doubt, or whatever else has come up in their reading.

Probability with Paulina

Sacred geometry is something my family firmly believed in, and the concept has been around for many centuries. My family said that even the world is on a grid of latitude and longitude, and we are guided by these sacred numbers. Sacred geometry is the belief that the universe, deities, spirit, or what have you is like an architect, and certain geometric shapes and proportions found in nature have symbolic and sacred meanings. These principles have been used in the design and construction of religious structures such as churches, temples, mosques, religious monuments, and altars, as well as in mandalas and other spiritual or religious art.

In the delicate balance of shapes and proportions, there's an inherent order that resonates with the universe. With its intricate patterns and symmetrical designs, sacred geometry is a bridge between the spiritual and the scientific. From the exploration of consciousness in quantum physics to the patterns found in nature's fractals, the connection between the tangible and the transcendental becomes ever more apparent. Telling the skeptic about the intersections of science and magic throughout history can also help to open their mind. Divination is the intersection where the ethereal meets the empirical. A lot of people like numbers. It's just another language they can relate to, and if they're skeptically minded, they may be more likely to respond to the language of probability. So it can also help to include a percentage in possible feelings or predictions that you feel like most accurately reflects your intuition and what you see in the divinatory tools you're using. For example, if you're reading for a person who's wondering what the year ahead might look like, and the tarot cards lay out The Tower, the Ace of Pentacles, and the Four of Wands, you might say to your client, "I feel there is a 70% chance you will be getting a new job or a promotion and have better financial foundations."

My mom and aunties taught me that if you're laying out a twelve- to fifteen-card general spread for a client, and it's the first spread of the reading, then whatever cards you pull have a high probability of playing out as the spread indicates, perhaps 80%. However, in my family, we believe that if the Wheel of Fortune comes up in the spread, especially in the first three cards, the probability drops to 50% because other people's free will in your client's life is influencing the unfolding of events, which makes everything cloudier and difficult to predict accurately. If the Wheel of Fortune is the last card in the spread, however, we read that as affecting the more distant future after the predicted outcome happens from the previous cards.

Venture into the world of chance in mathematics, and you find a surprising companion in the realm of gambling. The roll of a die, the shuffle of cards—the unpredictable nature of these games aligns with the unpredictable currents of destiny. It's a numerical ballet where probability and uncertainty intertwine, offering a glimpse into the mysterious ways in which mathematical laws mirror the enigmatic paths of fate. I tell clients that every time you shuffle the cards, you are creating a moment of chance. Just like you learn enough statistics to win at blackjack, and count cards to keep track of what's going on at the table, what comes out in your tarot reading is an opportunity for you to make the best of what chance lays out in front of you from the tarot deck. Like the butterfly effect, any number of things can happen from the choices you make or don't make, and any number of things could happen after that. Tarot is a randomized chance at insight, and this shuffle, this spread, is just for you. It's your choice whether or not you're going to bet on it. Are you feeling lucky?

But it's not just a matter of luck. It's what we do with our life that matters, and in that way, we can make our own luck too. Consider the art of manifestation—an endeavor where you harness the power of belief to bring your desires into reality, like programming the universe with your intentions. The alignment of your thoughts and actions increases the likelihood of a desired outcome in a cosmic pas de deux. But people can be skeptical of manifestation, and they should be. Many spiritual gurus say that you can visualize your way out of poverty and illness, which suggests that people who are oppressed by systems that limit their opportunities are just not spiritual enough to succeed, which is not true. Many mainstream teachings about manifestation are deeply flawed and can overlook real-life factors like racism, sexism, ableism, classism, homophobia, transphobia, and more.

At the same time, there is something to be gained from manifestation. When you continuously do something, like visualize your desired outcome, journal about it, pray on it, do a spell, or whatever you do to manifest, then the chances of you succeeding increase because it affects your behavior, the choices you make, the chances you take, and your belief in your ability, which increases your confidence. So suddenly mystical concepts seem very reasonable to the skeptic. Manifestation is just a piece of the puzzle.

Jung with Jezmina

I'm not much of a numbers person. I get bored partway through counting to ten. I'm much more intrigued by the way that fortune-telling is connected to our psychology. I'm no doctor and I don't pretend to be. However, archetypes and symbols are the language of psychology as well as divination, which makes sense because pioneers in Western psychology like Carl Jung were heavily influenced by Eastern beliefs and practices. The tarot cards are made up of twenty-two Major Arcana cards that represent states of being and major themes, like change, destruction, fate, and power, all of which are familiar to us as part of the human experience. The fifty-six cards in the Minor Arcana are more situational and deal with our personalities, struggles, and triumphs, the very fabric of the mundane. I like to tell my skeptical clients that the arrangement of cards is by chance, and we can decide to find meaning in them. Each card represents a facet of the human experience, and the shuffle, the choice of cards, the lay of the spread are all random. And yet, within the random, there are synchronicities and coincidences that create meaning, and maybe even offer good advice.

The same is true for tea-leaf or coffee reading, whose symbols like ink blots cannot be certain, but they evoke something in us. We name them like cloud shapes, and in naming the symbols, we create an opportunity for understanding, even if you're only humoring it as an exercise. And the palm, well, how interesting is it to understand the hills and valleys of your own hand and see the lines that change over time draw out what has been, what is, and what could be? Just as an experiment, what would it be like to see what the ancient art has to say about what all of this means, what's written on your body? It's up to you to decide what rings true for you. Usually even the most hardened skeptics find this a fun and stress-free approach that makes room for both their belief and disbelief, and centers them and their experience in the reading. I'm just relaying the information because I am the expert of the tools. They are the experts of their life.

Types of Skeptics

In the tapestry of fortune-telling and spirituality, recognizing various skeptical characters can help you navigate the reading with more confidence. Picture the Logical Luminary, armed with reason, the Evidential Explorer seeking tangible truths, the cautious Spiritual Seeker Skeptic, and the playful Cosmic Contrarian walking into your incense-laden shop and settling down before you. Engaging with these skeptics isn't just an exercise in connecting worlds; it's an opportunity for mutual discovery. By understanding and appreciating their perspectives, we transform skepticism from a barrier into a bridge, inviting them to open up to a new practice that they might actually love. Or maybe they don't love it, and that's okay too.

The Logical Luminary

As the door chimes, signaling the entrance of the Logical Luminary, you can almost hear the gears turning in their analytical mind. Armed with a healthy dose of skepticism and a penchant for logic, they approach your mystical realm like a detective solving a case. They want to know how it all works. Engage the Logical Luminary with a blend of grounded explanations and relatable anecdotes. They might like to understand the card meanings and their relationships, or the reasoning behind what you say. Showcase the ways in which simple spiritual practices can complement, rather than clash with, their logical worldview. For instance, practicing gratitude might be good for the soul, but studies show it does actually make people feel happier and more grounded. Invite them on a journey where intuition and reason walk hand in hand, unlocking the door to a world where the mystical and the rational converge.

The Evidential Explorer

With a raised eyebrow and a thirst for evidence, the Evidential Explorer steps into your sacred space, seeking tangible proof amidst the ethereal. They want proof that you're the real deal, that the divination tools yield results, and that they can trust what you say, and even then, that might not be enough. Cater to their curiosity by sharing stories of synchronicities and meaningful experiences that you have experienced yourself. Introduce them to the subtle art of interpreting signs and symbols, illustrating how the universe communicates in its own mysterious language. Ask them about their own connection to their intuition, and how they can learn to trust their own signs and signals. In embracing the unknown, the Evidential Explorer may find that sometimes the most profound truths are felt rather than seen.

The Spiritual Seeker Skeptic

Clad in flowing fabrics and adorned with crystals, the Spiritual Seeker Skeptic may surprise you with their cautious optimism. They've been burned before by false promises and charlatans, so approach them with sincerity and humility. Share the authenticity of your practice, emphasizing its roots in genuine connection and personal growth. Make it clear that they know themselves best, and you are just here to guide them toward a possible path, but they take the first step. This reading is not about predicting the future with certainty, but about navigating the present with wisdom. By fostering a space of trust and openness, you might help them rediscover the beauty of their own spiritual journey.

The Cosmic Contrarian

Draped in skepticism like a cloak, the Cosmic Contrarian enters your haven with a smirk, challenging the very fabric of your work. They want to knock you off your footing and your confidence. They might be teasing, or even confrontational. Embrace their playful skepticism with a bit of humor. Acknowledge the cosmic joke that life is full of uncertainty and the only certainty is change, and invite them to join in the fun by reminding them that it's just a reading. You're not here to prove anything. You're here to provide an experience, and they can make of it what they will. Frame the reading as an invitation to dance with the unknown rather than a rigid prescription of fate. By turning skepticism into a celestial waltz, you might just sway the Cosmic Contrarian into the rhythm of the reading.

Time to Be Professional

Dealing with skeptical clients politely and gracefully is the mark of professionalism. You can be a gifted reader but lack the skills to navigate more challenging clients, and your ability and reputation will suffer for it. Now that you have some tools to deal with our sometimes tricky but loveable clients, the skeptics, you're ready to consider the next step—the initiation of your own fortune-telling business. If you want to. You don't have to monetize all your hobbies and talents. But if that's your journey, we clear the path for you in the next chapter, How to Be a Professional.

CHAPTER 12

How to Be a Professional

We aren't experts in business, but we've both been reading professionally since we were kids. Paulina's family always had fortune-telling shops that they usually lived above, and Jezmina has enjoyed freelancing with a number of venues, agencies, and organizations. We're sharing a few tips for going professional.

Making Yourself Visible

Visibility doesn't have to be all online, though it helps to have an active social media so that you can build a following and so companies can tag you in events. You don't have to dedicate all your time to becoming an influencer, but it helps to produce some kind of content that people can connect to.

You should also have a website. It doesn't have to be fancy, but it helps to own your own domain name and have a place where people can easily find information about your reading style and training, your services, rates, and how to book with you. It makes it much easier to schedule clients, and it also makes you look much more professional. Ask people you've read for to give you testimonies for your website as well. It also helps to offer online or phone options so you can read for clients from anywhere. Visibility in the community, in person, is just as important as online visibility, however.

Book at Diverse Events

Make sure that you try reading at as many different venues, events, and parties as possible so that you're exposed to different clients. Order some attractive and informative business cards and carry them on you at all times. Be charming and inquisitive everywhere you go, because you never know where you're going to get your next job. You might strike up a chat with your hairdresser and next thing you know she's booking you for a private party at her salon. Offer to give talks at the library or local community clubs so you can share your craft with others and recruit clients that way. Step out of your comfort zone because you can find loyal clients anywhere.

Keeping Clients

Keep in touch with clients, but don't hit them up for business. This is where social media comes in handy, but you can also do this if you work in a shop and see them in person from time to time. It's okay to send them articles or other resources that you think would be helpful, or comment on their social media, especially if they're sharing a triumph or something you can encourage and support. Think of the relationship like friendly colleagues. You're not getting personal with them, but you're staying connected in a positive, supportive, yet boundaried way.

Developing Your Style

This is part branding and part knowing yourself. This is where all the awareness of lineage, training, personal experience, cultural influence, personal style, and expertise all converge. Developing your style requires that you know how to market yourself and explain what you do. It also requires that you have an aesthetic that stays consistent with how you dress, decorate your space, design your business cards and website, and more. It's owning what makes you unique.

Conclusion

While we initially wrote this as a fortune-telling book, we realized through our writing that this is also a guide for survival in a tough world. Fortune-telling is about reading people, being a good listener, believing your intuition, navigating challenges, finding solutions, and always learning. Roma have persisted through the centuries against all odds with many different skills and trades, and fortune-telling is just one of them. The two of us, however, have overcome trauma and obstacles that we thought would surely break us, and yet, partly due to our trade, we learned to adapt, read the room, roll with fate, take opportunities, and trust our instincts. Everything we have, we owe to what we've learned from our families, and whether the lesson was to follow them or break those cycles, we learned to trust ourselves first. We hope that our stories and experiences help you relate to us not just as fortune-tellers but as humans, whether you're Romani or gadje, and help you know yourself better too.

Appendix

Romani Organizations and Resources for Further Education

Romanistan Podcast

Romatopia Podcast

Roma Unraveled Podcast

Amaro Voice Podcast

O Verda Darano Podcast

Roma Peoples Project at Columbia University

The Roma Program at Harvard University

ERIAC (European Roma Institute for Arts and Culture)

ERRC (European Roma Rights Centre)

RomArchive

E-Romnja

Giuvlipen

The Foundation towards Dialogue (Fundacja w Stronę Dialogu)

Traveller Pride

Phiren Amenca

Dikh He Na Bister

World Roma Federation

Movimento Kethane

Voice of Roma

Romano Lav

Lolo Diklo

Travellers Times

Friends, Families, and Travellers

Ververipen

Romedia Foundation

Glossary

baxt: good luck, good fortune, happiness

bibaxt: bad luck, misfortune

BIPOC: an acronym for Black, Indigenous, People of Color

cezve: a small, long-handled pot with a lip, designed for making Turkish coffee

dikk: Romani word for look (also dikhel)

Dom: The Dom are descendants of the Dom caste with roots in India, and while the Dom people were formerly grouped with other Indian diaspora groups, like the Romani and Lom people, the Dom do not identify as Romani. They are mostly settled in the Middle East/West Asia, and North Africa.

drabimos: fortune-telling (also drabarimos, and dukkering)

dukkerer: fortune-teller (also drabarni)

evil eye: also known as the nazar, ayin hara, malocchio, mal de ojo, jakheli. It a common and ancient belief across many cultures that a glance can cause illness, harm, bad luck, or even death. Sometimes people cast the evil eye purposefully, or as a result of their envy or malice, and other times it can be totally accidental. Usually pregnant women, babies, and animals are the most vulnerable, but everyone is susceptible.

gadje: the Romani word for non-Romani people. Gadjo is the singular masculine form, gadji is the singular feminine form, and gadje is the plural form.

Giuvlipen: the Romani word for feminism, also the name for the feminist Romani theater troupe, Giuvlipen, founded in 2014 by Mihaela Drăgan and Zita Moldovan.

Gypsy: a term referring to the Romani people, sometimes used for other historically nomadic people, whether nomadic by force or choice. The word Gypsy comes from the inaccurate belief that Roma are originally from India. Gypsy is used as a racial slur, and has been historically, and references stereotypes of criminality, nomadism, magicality, and sexuality. Some Roma reclaim this word personally, but still prefer that non-Roma, or gadje, not use it. Some Roma, especially in the UK and Ireland, see the word as neutral and are comfortable with non-Roma using it to refer to them, as it is a legal category in that part of the world. Some are not comfortable with it and see it as a racial slur. Either way, because it is a racially charged word for so many, it is important for non-Roma not to use it or appropriate the word Gypsy, and to defer to Roma for how they would like to be identified.

jakheli: the Romani word for evil eye

jakhendar: the ritual process of removing the evil eye

Lom: the Lom are a diasporic ethnic group with origins in India who are mostly settled in Armenia, Georgia, Turkey, and surrounding areas. They are related to Roma but do not always identify as Roma.

marime: dirty, unclean, soiled, outcast

Muchwaya/Machwaya: a Romani subgroup that had mainly settled in Serbia and the Austro-Hungarian Empire

prikaza: bad luck, misfortune

Roma/Rroma: (noun) the diasporic ethnic group with origins in Northern India, who left India in waves circa 1000 CE. Rroma is an alternate spelling for Roma.

Roma Futurism: an artistic movement blending Romani culture with technology and witchcraft, and combining elements of science fiction, Romani history, fantasy, Roma subjectivity, magical realism, creative technology, magical practices, and healing rituals. Roma Futurism was pioneered by Mihaela Drăgan and Giuvlipen and has influenced contemporary Romani art and literature.

Romani/Romany/Rromani: (adjective) referring to or describing the Roma people, culture, or language

Romanipen: the Romani way of life; spiritual, social, and cultural rules, laws, or practices that Roma are expected to follow

Romanistan: the name of an imaginary country where all Roma belong. Romanistan was at one time a proposition for a real country, which the authors do not support. Instead, Romanistan is the global community of Roma united in camaraderie, which the authors do support.

Sara la Kali: (also known as Kali Sara, Sara Kali, Saint Sarah, The Black Madonna, and other names): the Romani goddess/saint who likely finds her origins in the Hindu goddess Kali and evolved over time to be the benevolent protector of the Romani people.

Sinti: a subgroup of Romani people settled mostly in Germany, France, Italy, and Central Europe. They arrived in these parts of Europe earlier than other Romani subgroups and were hit particularly hard by the genocide of WWII, so the population has been severely diminished. The Sinti of Central Europe are closely related to the group known as Manouche in France. The Sinti are often referred to as separate from Roma even though they are related.

tasseomancy: (also known as tasseography, tassology, or tasseology): a method of divination or fortune-telling that interprets tea leaves, coffee grounds, or wine sediments

Techno Witch: The Techno Witch or Cyber Witch is the main figure of Roma Futurism, created by Mihaela Drăgan, and is a character or archetype in Roma Futurist art and literature with the superpower to transcend time and to intervene in the oppressive past of their own Roma community with the goal to change it. They travel to specific moments in time with the purpose of creating alternative histories.

Traveller, or Irish Traveller: the traditionally nomadic ethnic minority indigenous to Ireland properly known as the Mincéir. While they are ethnically and culturally different from Roma, sometimes Travellers are referred to as Gypsies as well, and sometimes Roma might call themselves Travellers.

vitsa: a Romani word that describes subgroups or clans of Roma. It can refer to large subgroups, like the Muchwaya, Kalderash, Lovari, etc. But vitsa also refers to large extended families related through a matrilineal or patrilineal ancestor that share a name group, and may travel together or otherwise maintain very close community connection.

yoks: Anglo-Romani word meaning eyes

About the Authors

Jezmina Von Thiele (they/she) is a writer, educator, performer, and fortune-teller in their mixed Sinti Romani tradition. Their poetry, fiction, and nonfiction has been published in *Prairie Schooner, The Kenyon Review Online, Narrative Magazine,* and elsewhere under the name Jessica Reidy. Jezmina reads tarot, palms, and tea leaves. They also teach classes and workshops on divination, spiritual wellness, and the creative arts. Jezmina often tells fortunes and performs poetry with *The Poetry Brothel,* Boston's premiere immersive literary event. Jezmina is also cohost of *Romanistan,* a podcast celebrating Romani culture, and owner and operator of the online vintage shop, Evil Eye Edit. Jezmina is based in Portsmouth, New Hampshire.

Paulina Stevens, rooted in a Muchwaya Romani heritage of fortune-telling and healing, has blended ancestral wisdom with modern holistic practices. Her expertise in tarot, palmistry, and energy healing forms the foundation of her comprehensive wellness coaching. Paulina serves clients globally, offering personalized guidance incorporating spirituality, herbalism, and fortune-telling online and at her California-based private practice, Romani Holistic. Paulina is the subject of the *LA Times* podcast *Foretold.* The podcast follows Paulina as she navigates the consequences of her decision to leave her arranged marriage and community to redefine her identity. She is the cohost of *Romanistan,* a podcast that educates, empowers, and celebrates Romani culture, outcasts, rebels, and revolutionaries. Paulina is based in Los Angeles.

To Our Readers

Weiser Books, an imprint of Red Wheel/Weiser, publishes books across the entire spectrum of occult, esoteric, speculative, and New Age subjects. Our mission is to publish quality books that will make a difference in people's lives without advocating any one particular path or field of study. We value the integrity, originality, and depth of knowledge of our authors.

Our readers are our most important resource, and we appreciate your input, suggestions, and ideas about what you would like to see published.

Visit our website at *www.redwheelweiser.com*, where you can learn about our upcoming books and free downloads, and also find links to sign up for our newsletter and exclusive offers.

You can also contact us at *info@rwwbooks.com* or at

Red Wheel/Weiser, LLC
65 Parker Street, Suite 7
Newburyport, MA 01950